C0-ARJ-798

THE PRIMA DONNA

THE
PRIMA DONNA

Anonymous

Carroll & Graf Publishers, Inc.
New York

First Carroll & Graf edition 1984

ISBN: 0-88184-088-2

Carroll & Graf Publishers, Inc.
260 Fifth Avenue
New York, N.Y. 10001

Printed in the United States of America

THE PRIMA DONNA

PART ONE

I

Why hide anything from you? You have always been a true and disinterested friend. In life's hardest situations, you have served me in such important ways that now I can certainly confide in you completely. Besides, your wish does not surprise me; in our talks in former times, I often noticed your great desire to scrutinize and understand the secret springs which, in us women, are the motives for so many actions that even the most sensitive of men are hard put to explain them.

Circumstances have separated us now and we shall probably never see each other again. I often think very gratefully of how you helped me in my great misfortune. In all you have done for me, you never thought of your own interest, you were only occupied with mine. It depended only on yourself to obtain all the marks of favor a man could desire; you knew my temperament, and I had a weakness for you.

Opportunities were not lacking for us and I often admired your self-control. I know you are as sensitive as myself on this point; you often repeated to me that I had a penetrating eye and more reason than most women. You are convinced of this, or you would not ask me to communicate with you, without circumlocution and with no false feminine modesty (which I believe most women affect, in any case), my experiences and my conception of thought and feeling in woman, in relation to the most important moment of her life, love and her union with man. At first your wish upset me, for — allow me to begin this confession by exposing a very characteristic one — nothing is harder for us than to be completely sincere with a man. Customs and social constraint oblige us from our youth to be very prudent, and we cannot be frank without danger.

When I had thought carefully about what you asked of me, and above all when I had remembered all the qualities of the man who was writing to me, your idea began to amuse me. I tried telling some of my experiences. Certain things, demanding an absolute sincerity and which precisely it is not the custom to express, still made me hesitate. But I made an effort, thinking to please you, and allowed myself to be invaded by the memory of the happy hours that I have tasted. At heart, I only regret one of them, the one whose unfortunate consequences led me to resort to your friendship, in order not to succumb to it. After this first hesitation, I felt a tremendous joy in relating all I have lived, in person, and that other women have experienced. My blood stirred in the most agreeable fashion as I summoned up the smallest details. It was like savoring again the pleasures I have tasted and of which I am not ashamed, as you well know.

Our relationship has been so intimate that it would be ridiculous of me to want to show myself in a false light; but apart from you and the unhappy wretch who betrayed me so miserably, no one knows me. Thanks to my sense of the practical, I have always managed to hide my inner self. This is due to a succession of extraordinary causes rather than to my own merit.

In the circle of my acquaintances, I have the reputation of being a virtuous woman, even cold. Yet on the contrary, few women have so rejoiced in their body until their thirty-sixth year. To what purpose this long preface? I send you what I have written these last days; you yourself will judge to what degree I have been sincere. I have tried to answer your first question, and I have convinced myself of your assertion, that sexual character is formed by special circumstances wherein are unveiled the veiled mysteries of love; I think that such has been my case.

I am zealously continuing these confessions; however, you will not receive a second letter before having replied to the present one. Meanwhile, this equivocal way of writing amuses me more than I would have believed. Your noble character is a guarantee you will not abuse my confidence. What would I have become without you, without your friendship and without your precious advice? A poor thing, miserable, solitary and dishonored in the eyes of the world; but then I know you have a little love for me, in spite of your apparent coldness and your disinterestedness. Believe me, etc., etc.

Dresden, Feb. 7, 1851.

II

My parents, comfortable but possessed of no great fortune, gave me an exemplary education. Thanks to my vivacious character, to my great facility in learning and my early-developed musical talent, I was the spoilt child of our house, the favorite of all our acquaintances.

My temperament had not yet revealed itself. In my thirteenth year, I learned from other young girls of the difference between the masculine and feminine sex, and they told me also that the tale of the stork who brought children was a fable and that strange and mysterious things must happen at marriage; but I lent no more than the interest of idle curiosity to these sayings. My senses took no part in it. It was only on the first signs of puberty, when a light fleece of curly hair appeared in that place which my mother never permitted me completely to expose, even during my toilet, that certain agreeable feelings mingled with this curiosity. When I was alone, I examined this incomprehensible growth of tiny hairs and the surroundings of this precious area that I suspected of possessing such great importance, the world hid it and veiled it so carefully. When I got up, when I knew I was alone behind closed doors, I unhooked a mirror, I placed it before me and inclined it so as to be able to see everything distinctly. With my fingers I opened what nature had so carefully closed, understanding less and less what my friends had told me of the way in which the most intimate union of man and woman is accomplished. I saw that it was all impossible. I had seen from statues the different way in which nature had endowed man. In this way I examined myself, when I washed myself in cold water during the week, when I was naked and alone, for on Sunday, in my mother's presence, I had to be covered from hip to knee. My attention also was soon attracted by the ever-growing roundness of my breasts, by

18

the ever more ample form of my hips and thighs. This realization gave me an incomprehensible pleasure. I grew dreamy. I would attempt in the strangest of ways to explain to myself what I could never understand. I remember well that my vanity began at this period. It was also at that time that in the evening, in bed, I surprised myself, in surprising my hand unconsciously making its way across my lower belley, where it would play with the newly growing hairs. The heat of my hand amused me, but I did not then suspect all that still lay dormant in that place. Habitually I would close my thighs over my hand and fall asleep in that attitude.

My father was an austere man and my mother a model of feminine virtue and good behavior. And so I honored them much and loved them passionately. My father never joked and never, in my presence, offered a tender word to my mother; they were both of fine appearance. My father was about forty years old, my mother thirty-four.

I would never have believed that under such a serious outward appearance, and such dignified behavior, was hidden so much secret sensuality and such appetites for pleasure. Chance instructed me.

I was fourteen years old and undergoing religious tuition towards my confirmation. I had, like all my companions, an exalted love for our pastor. I have often noticed since then that the teacher, and particularly the religious teacher, is the first man to make a lasting impression on young girls. If his sermon is understandable and if he is a prominent man in the neighborhood, all his young pupils become infatuated with him. I shall return to this point, since it is on your list of questions.

I was therefore fourteen years of age, my body was fully developed even to that essential mark of womanhood — the flowering of the period. My father's birthday was approaching. My mother lovingly made all the preparations. Early in the morning I was already in my party dress, for my father liked fine clothes. I had written a poem, you know of my talent for verse — between ourselves, my verses were corrected by the pastor, which gave me a pretext for going to see him — I had picked a posy of flowers.

My parents did not share a room. My father often worked far into the night and did not want to disturb my mother; at least that is what he said. Later on, I recognized in this yet another obvious sign of their wise way of life. Married couples should avoid as much as possible letting themselves sink into a routine. All the fuss consequent on getting up and going to bed, indifference, the evening toilet, are often ridiculous, spoil many charms and communal life loses its attraction. My father therefore never slept in my mother's room. Usually he got up at seven o'clock.

On his birthday, my mother got up at six to get the presents ready and to decorate my father's portrait. Towards seven o'clock, she complained of being tired and said she was going to lie down for a while, until my father awoke.

Heaven knows where I got the idea, but I thought it would be nice to surprise my father in my mother's room and give him his birthday wishes there. I had heard him coughing in his room. He was therefore already up and would soon come in. While my mother gave her last orders to the servant, I slipped into her bedroom and hid behind the glass doors of an alcove that served us for a wardrobe. Proud and happy about my plan, I stayed breathless behind the glass door, when my mother came in. Rapidly she undressed to her petticoat, sat on the low toilet basin and carefully washed herself. For the first time I saw my mother's fine body. She adjusted a large mirror at the foot of the bed, near the toilet basin, and lay down, her eyes on the door. Then I understood the indelicacy I had committed; I would have liked to disappear from the alcove. A presentiment warned me that things were about to happen before my eyes that a young girl ought not to see. I held my breath and trembled in all my limbs. Suddenly, the door opened, my father came in, dressed as usual every morning, in an elegant dressing gown. The door had hardly moved when my mother quickly closed her eyes and pretended to be asleep. My father went up to the bed and gazed at my "sleeping" mother with an expression of great tenderness. Then he went and locked the door. I trembled more and more, I wanted the earth to swallow me up. My father slid off his trousers. Now he was in his shirt under his gown. He went over to the bed and carefully drew off the light blanket. Now I know well that it was not mere accident, as I innocently thought at the time, that my mother was lying with her thighs wide apart, one leg bent and the other outstretched. For the first time I saw another woman's body, but full and in fine flower, and I thought with shame of my own, still so green. The petticoat was folded back, nothing was hidden, one round white breast emerged from the lace.

Later on I met few women who would have

dared so to present themselves to their husband or to their lover.

My father's eyes drank in this spectacle. Then he leaned gently over the sleeping one, moistened his finger at his mouth and carried it to the point from which he could not take his eyes. He drew it delicately up and down. My mother sighed, then she raised the other leg and began to make strange movements of the hip. The blood climbed to my face; I was ashamed. I wanted to turn my eyes away, but I could not. The movements of the hips quickened, my father moistened the finger a second time, then he drove it in so deeply that his hand seemed to lose itself in the thick curly fleece. At that moment my mother opened her eyes, as if she had just woken up with a start and, violently closing her thighs on my father's now captive hand, she said with a deep sigh:

"Is it you, my dear? I was dreaming of you that very instant. What a pleasant way to wake me! Many, many happy returns on your birthday."

"The best of all is to surprise you like this. How beautiful you are today! You should have seen yourself!"

"And to surprise me when I least expect you! Have you locked the door?"

"Don't be afraid. But if you really want to wish me happiness, open your thighs again. You are fresh and perfumed as a dewy rose!"

"I will give you anything, beloved. But don't you want to wait till evening?"

"You shouldn't have shown yourself in such a tantalizing way. There, feel there, you can see for yourself I can't wait any longer."

And he bent over her, and there was no end to

the kissing. But his hand was still in the same place, more lovingly, more caressingly than ever, and I saw my mother's hand glide furtively under her husband's dressing gown. The kisses grew more ardent. My father kissed her neck, her breasts, he sucked the little rosy nipples, he went lower and concentrated his kisses on that center of all feminine graces. When my mother felt this contact, she threw herself across the bed. My father knelt down. He parted her thighs with his two hands and not for a moment did his lips leave the source of his pleasure. Since he had his back to me, I could not see what he was doing, but I concluded from the little exclamations my mother uttered that she felt an extraordinary pleasure. Her eyes brimmed with tears, her breasts trembled, her thighs shivered. She sighed convulsively:

"Oh, that's wonderful! A little higher! How good you are! Suck, suck! like that! It's coming! Oh! why can't I kiss you, too! Heaven! A little lower with the tongue! Quicker! Ah! ah! it's coming! I . . . ah . . . stop! It's too much! Oh, it's good! Ah . . . "

Each of these words is fixed in my memory. How many times have I said them to myself! What they have made me think and dream about! I seem still to hear them in my ears. And what I also heard was a sound like a tiny fart . . . I think it was released by my mother.

There was a moment's pause. My mother stayed immobile, eyes closed, body spread, thighs resting on the edge of the bed. No longer did I have before me a severe father, a dignified and virtuous mother. I saw two people knowing no convention anymore, flinging themselves, overcome, drunken, into the ardors of a pleasure I did not know. For a moment my father stayed still, then sat down on the edge of the bed. A savage look burned in his eyes, he could not turn away from what he so desired. My mother was moaning sensuously. During this spectacle, I gasped for breath, I was suffocating, my heart was beating too fast. A thousand thoughts awoke in my head, and I was very apprehensive, not knowing how to leave my hiding place without being seen. My uncertainty did not last, for what I had just seen was only a preamble. In what followed I was to learn enough in a single experience never again to have need of a lesson.

My father sat down beside my outstretched mother. Now his face was turned towards me. He must have been hot, for suddenly he took off both shirt and dressing gown. And so I saw all at once what had given me, in the tales of my friends, the greatest food for thought.

I was almost crying, I was so excited by curiosity. How different it was from little boys and statues. I very well remember that I was afraid and that, nonetheless, a delicious shiver ran up my back. My father still had his eyes on my mother; with one hand, he seemed to be controlling his rebellious member, for he was caressing it softly and I saw him bare the end. I shook more and more and, as if something were about to happen to me, I held my thighs gripped closely together.

I already knew from my friends that these two parts exposed to my sight for the first time belonged to each other. But how was that possible? I could not understand, for it appeared to me that their size was out of all proportion. After a few instants' pause, my father took my mother's inanimate hand and guided it to what so irresistibly drew my eyes. When she felt what he placed in her hand, she opened her eyes, smiled blissfully and threw herself with such passion at my father's lips that I understood I had seen no more than the innocent preliminaries of what was about to happen. They did not speak, but after having exchanged the most burning of kisses, and while my father's hand was still between my mother's thighs, they undressed each other completely.

Then my mother lay back on a heap of cushions that raised her hind quarters and I saw she was rocking from side to side; at last she found the most favorable position, allowing her easily to watch the reflection of the mirror she had leaned against the foot of the bed before my father had come in. My father did not notice it, for he was looking less at the beautifully sparkling face of my mother than at her thighs. These were now very wide apart. My father knelt between them. I saw it all clearly. I thought my eyes would burst, they were so swollen with curiosity. Then my mother took her husband's proud lance and let it to that marvelous opening, moistening it with saliva, and rubbing herself in the same place several times, up and down, and at the same time uttering sighs. Then she said:

"Softly, dear, we must have it together. The first flow was so full that the second won't come so quickly. Don't leave me on the way!"

Poor ignorant girl that I was, what could I understand of what my mother said? I saw my father's member disappear into its lodging place. Instead of crying out with pain, as I expected, my mother's eyes shone with pleasure. She knotted her two legs round my father's back to help it in more deeply. Her fervent eyes followed my father's every movement in the mirror. The numberless feelings that agitated me then prevented me from realizing that these two interwoven bodies were very beautiful. I know now that such beauty is very rare. When my father had fully penetrated her, after a few minutes of immobility, my mother slightly loosed the grip of her thighs. He straightened up then, withdrawing the fiery arrow to plunge it in again to its roots. My mother rocked her hips, moved towards him. At each movement, their pleasure seemed to increase. Unfortunately I could not see my father's face, but at his ever more frantic movements, I felt that a drunkenness was overtaking him. He did not speak, he only moved. My mother, on the contrary, uttered incoherent words, that allowed me, however, to grasp what was going on between them:

"There, deeper, beloved! Right to the end. No, more slowly. Ah! How strong you are today! Is it good? I'm still soaked from the first flow, you must like that! Quicker now! There! Oh! That's good! You aren't ready yet, are you? Deeper! Ah! Ah! Oh, what a shame, you're done already and I'm not there! What a flood! I felt it go up to my heart!"

My father still said nothing. His movements quickened. He seemed to have lost all control of himself. There was not the slightest pause between going in and coming out. Contortions gripped his body. He panted, trembled, his thighs shivered nervously. Finally, he thrust himself in so deeply that he quite covered my mother, motionless as if dead, her head slumped on the swelling of her breast. Then, exhausted, he turned on his side. My mother took a towel, and while she wiped herself I was able to see the change that had come about in them both. What in my father had been so huge, red and threatening was now very small, tiny, limp, the end covered with a white liquid that my mother wiped away. But what had been so tightly closed and hardly visible in my mother was now wide open, prominent, inflamed and red. A white liquid was pouring from it as if the whole cavern had been filled; and I, foolish thing that I was, could not understand where it might possibly have come from. My mother took some water, and first washed my father very tenderly, then took a little syringe with a curving nozzle, which she filled, and pushing it into herself washed herself thoroughly inside.

At last she lay back beside my father, motionless and dreaming. He seemed satisfied. Not so my mother. She seemed to be prey to the same excitement that had seized her when he had kissed her between the thighs. In completing her toilet, she had straightened the mirror as if by accident, and my father, now at his place on the pillow, could not see the reflection which had given her such pleasure. I had followed the scene so carefully that not even this little movement escaped me, but I was not to understand it until much later. I thought it was all over now. My senses were violently disturbed, and almost hurt me. And I was thinking how to escape without betraying my presence, but I was still to see more. Seated at his feet, my mother leaned over my father, kissed him, and asked him tenderly:

"Are you happy?"

"More than ever, you adorable woman. But I

am sorry you didn't end with me. I was too excited. I couldn't restrain myself. It flowed like a fountain."

"It doesn't matter. On your birthday, it's only your pleasure I care about. And besides, the first time it was divine."

And so saying, she bent over him and began to kiss the place she had so adored in herself. Now I saw much better what was happening.

First she kissed only the outside, stroked it, petted it, then took the whole of the end in her mouth while my father's face contorted in spasms of ecstasy. He first pinched her breasts with his right hand, then moved it between her voluptuous thighs, which immediately parted to give him more room. I saw his finger move in her font, then slide in slowly and penetrate completely while she, with her mouth, was more and more avid. Finally, O wonder! her caresses succeeded in once more bringing to life the charming little thing which now lifted itself and again took on the form I had first seen. My mother had succeeded in her task, and her eyes shone with desire. As my father remained immobile, visibly satisfied by the pleasing occupation of his hand, she mounted him suddenly, and my father's body lay between her widespread thighs.

As it happened, everything was arranged to my advantage. I could see all that took place twice: once in the bed, the side of which was facing me, and the second time from behind, in the mirror. That which, up until now, I had only been able to partially distinguish, I could now see fully and as distinctly as if I had been taking part. I shall never forget this spectacle. It was as beautiful as I could possibly desire, and far

28

more beautiful than any of those in which I subsequently took part. The pair were in perfect health, strong, and immensely excited. My mother was now active while my father was much calmer than before. He clasped her round white hips, letting one of his fingers stray into her brown and hairy anus, then took the nipple of one of her breasts between his lips and sucked it whenever she leaned too far forward. However, his abdomen hardly moved. My mother, on the contrary, was on fire and was writhing feverishly. With her hand she directed the menacing lance toward her opening and threw herself on it, absorbing it to the root. What I had seen before had filled me with consternation and fear. Now other feelings swept over me. It was troubled and filled with a strange, sweet sensation. If I had not been afraid of crumpling my dress, I should have immediately put my hand there where my mother seemed to feel this overwhelming pleasure. She had forgotten everything—this serious and self-possessed woman—and was caught up in a whirlwind of pleasure. The sight defied description. My father's strong limbs, my mother's round, dazzlingly white curves and, above all, those parts so closely joined, trembling as if all the life force of these two ecstatic beings was concentrated in them. When my mother rolled to one side I could see the ruby lips of her font separate reluctantly, parted from the virile scepter which, clasped closely between them, penetrated now to the depths, now appeared naked only to disappear again almost at once.

Now my mother was silent. Both seemed to feel the same degree of pleasure and both began to move more and more quickly, their eyes closing at the same time. Then, at the moment of supreme ecstasy, my father pushed his body upwards hard, as if to completely penetrate my mother's sweet haven, while she, opening her thighs even wider, pressed her body down in an effort to absorb everything into herself. My father began shouting, "I'm coming, I'm coming! It's going to spurt, I can't hold it!" And at the same moment my mother cried, "Oh yes, yes! I can feel the jet. Oh! It's wonderful!" Their delight lasted another moment or two before they fell back, entwined in each other's arms on the bed, and pulled up the cover to protect themselves from a chill, and so the sight of their bodies was hidden from me.

I was as if turned to stone. The two people for whom, until now, I had felt such love and respect had just revealed to me things about which young girls have the most absurd ideas. They had thrown off all dignity and had shown me that the world, under the mantle of respectability, seeks nothing but pleasure and sensuality. But I am not here to philosophize. My task is merely to narrate.

For about ten minutes they lay under the covers like dead things. After they finally got up, my father playfully slapped his wife's soft, round buttocks two or three times before they got dressed and left the bedroom. I knew that my mother was going to take him to the room where she'd laid out his presents. This room opened onto the veranda leading to the garden. After a few minutes, I furtively slipped from my hiding place and hurried into the garden to greet my parents. I still don't know how I managed to say my poem and wish my father happy birthday. Fortunately, he took my confusion for affection. However, I didn't dare look at my parents, for I couldn't forget the sight I had just witnessed. The image of their transports was still dancing before my eyes. My father and my mother kissed me in turn, but what different kisses these were from the ones they had exchanged such a few minutes before! I was so upset and confused that in the end my parents noticed it. I was dying with impatience to get back to my room to be alone and to go more deeply into what I had just learned, and I wanted to make a few experiments on my own account. My head was feverish and my blood throbbed wildly in my veins.

My mother, thinking that I was too tightly corseted, sent me up to my room. It gave me a splendid opportunity to undress, and this I did with such speed that I almost tore my clothes. How ugly my angular body seemed in comparison with her ample beauty. Where she was in the full bloom of womanhood, I was scarcely rounded, and her thick bush of hair was, on me, only a light down. Nevertheless, I decided to try on myself what I'd seen my father do to her. I rubbed from left, from right, then up and down. I parted as much as possible the lips of my orifice, but I couldn't get a finger in without a terrible pain. However, when my finger was moistened with saliva and I rubbed gently from above near the orifice, I felt a very pleasant sensation. I couldn't understand how such a feeling could unleash such delirium as to make one feel half senseless. I concluded that one could only reach such supreme ecstasy with the help of a man. I compared the pastor with my father. Was he as hot-blooded, as wild when he was alone with a woman? Would he be like that with me if I were ready to do what my mother had done? I could not yet forget that most beautiful scene in which my mother had reawakened with her caresses the sleeping desire of my father's body, had taken his lance into her mouth, and had kissed it so long and so ardently that it had stood once again stiff and had later disappeared inside her.

In less than an hour I had lived ten years. But when I saw that all my attempts on myself were in vain I gave up, exhausted, and began to ponder what I should try next. I was already a very methodical child and kept a diary where I noted all my little accounts, and where I wrote down all of my observations. I at once opened it and copied the words I had heard, but on separate pages so that no one would be able to understand these broken fragments. Then I began to think over what I had seen and I abandoned myself to reverie.

First of all, my mother had pretended to be asleep and, by her provocative attitude, had obliged my father to satisfy her desire. She had carefully hidden her wishes from him, trying to give the impression that she was condescending to give him something. Then she had also arranged the mirror in such a way as to double her own pleasure secretly. What I had seen myself in the mirror had also caused me more pleasure than the mere reality; I had distinctly seen there things which, without it, would have been hidden from me. She had made all these preparations without my father's knowledge, so I concluded that she didn't want to admit to him that she derived more pleasure from the act than he; she had even asked him if he wouldn't prefer to wait until the evening—she, who had prepared everything to satisfy their desires.

Secondly, both had shouted, "I'm coming! I'm coming!" They had also spoken of a jet, and at the moment of ecstasy they had cried together of its flowing. What were they talking about? I could come to no conclusion. You can't imagine all the stupid explanations I thought of. It's surprising that, in spite of their natural cunning, young girls grope about in the shadows for so long and discover so rarely the simplest and most natural explanations.

It was obvious that the kisses and the fondling were not the most important part of the play, but were intended to excite, although my mother had then seemed to feel the greatest pleasure. My father's caresses had made her cry out, "Deeper!" She had probably desired his tongue to enter farther and more completely.

In short, my thoughts were so jumbled and tormented that I could not calm myself all day. I didn't want to ask questions of anyone. Since my parents did these things in secret, I supposed it was forbidden to speak of them.

A lot of visitors came during the day, and in the afternoon my uncle arrived. He was accompanied by his wife, by my cousin, a girl of sixteen, and by a governess who came from French Switzerland. They spent the night at our house because my uncle had things to do in town the next day. My cousin and her governess shared my room. The girl was to share my bed, but I should have preferred to sleep with the governess, for whom they put up a camp bed. She was about twenty-eight years old, very vivacious, and had an answer for everything. She would probably have been able to tell me a lot. I didn't know how to set about it though, because she was very strict with my cousin. However, I would have relied on the intimacy of the night and on chance. I worked out a hundred schemes. When we went up to our room Marguerite the governess was ˙already there and had put a screen between our beds. She made us hurry to get to bed, listened to us say our prayers, wished us good night, told us to go to sleep quickly and took the lamp to her part of the room. She hardly needed to tell my cousin these things because the girl fell asleep as soon as her head touched the pillow. However I was restless. A thousand thoughts crowded through my head. I could hear Marguerite moving about, undressing and getting ready for the night. Then I noticed a feeble ray of light coming through a tiny hole in the screen. I leaned out of bed, made the hole bigger with a hairpin, and peeped through it. I could see Marguerite just getting into her nightdress.

Her body was not as lovely as my mother's, but her figure was round and full. Her breasts were small and firm and her thighs well shaped. I'd only been watching her a moment or two when she pulled up her nightdress. She took a book out of a bag lying on the table, sat down on the edge of the bed, and began reading. Soon she got up and, taking the lamp, came around to our side to see if we were asleep. I closed my eyes as hard as I could and didn't open them again until the governess had sat down on a chair. Then I watched her through the rip in the screen once more. Marguerite was reading intently. There must have been something unusual about the book, because her eyes were bright and her cheeks flushed. Her chest was heaving and suddenly she put her hand under her nightdress and, placing her foot on the edge of the bed, began to read more intently and with obvious delight. I couldn't see what her hand was doing under her gown, but I immediately thought of what I had seen that morning. Sometimes her fingers seemed to be playing and tangling in the hairs, and she quickly pressed her thighs together and began to squirm on her chair.

I was so engrossed by these occupations that I did not at first notice an alcohol lamp on the table. It was lighted and some liquid was steaming on it. I suppose she had lit it before I came into the room. She dipped her finger into the liquid to see if it was warm enough, and when she removed it I saw that the liquid was milk. Then she took a bundle of linen out of her bag, opened it, and unwrapped a strange, curiously-shaped object, the use of which I could not imagine. It was black and almost the same shape as the part of my father I had first seen that morning. She dipped it into the milk and tried it on her cheek to see if it was hot enough. Finally, she dipped the end of it into the milk again, pressed the two knobs at the other end, and filled the instrument with hot milk. She sat down, put her legs on the bed right opposite me, so that I could see straight between her legs, pulled up her nightdress, and picked up the book in her left hand. I had just time to catch a glimpse of some pictures without really being able to see what they represented. She seized the instrument in her right hand and put the end of it in that admirable place which I also was holding with both hands under my nightdress. She rubbed it slowly up and down and very gently on some particularly sensitive spot. Her eyes shone and seemed literally to absorb the pictures in the book. At last she found the entry for her instrument and slowly pushed in the whole of its barrel. Her thighs were now even further apart, her abdomen, which advanced convulsively to the meeting, offered itself, and Marguerite uttered a sigh of pleasure. She pushed in the instrument as far as possible and the two round knobs buried themselves in the thickness of her hair. Then she drew it out again with the same care, and she was now repeating this movement more and more quickly, more and more feverishly, until the book fell to the floor. She closed her eyes and rubbed a finger across her lips. The movements of the instrument grew more and more rapid until her body seemed to swoon. She bit her lips cruelly as if to smother a cry which would have betrayed her. The supreme moment had arrived. She pressed the knobs with both hands and the milk flooded out inside her. She closed her thighs on the instrument, which was embedded in her body, and remained without moving, only quivering slightly, profoundly shaken. At length, she opened her thighs, withdrew the instrument, which was covered with foam, and when the milk flooded out she caught it in her cloth. She wiped everything very carefully, packed the instrument away in her bag, and came around to see once again if we were asleep. Then she got into bed and soon went to sleep herself, with a happy and satisfied expression.

I couldn't sleep, however. If I was glad to have the solution to certain enigmas which had been worrying my little head since that morning, I was also exasperated. I made up my mind to question Marguerite. She would solve my problem, explain to me, help me. Once again a thousand schemes crowded my head, and my next letter will tell you how I carried them out.

Have I been frank enough?

III

Marguerite was my only hope. I would have liked to have gone around to her side of the screen and to have crawled into her bed. I would have threatened and implored her until she would have had to admit and explain to me these strange, forbidden, exciting things I had discovered today. She would have taught me how to imitate them, which was what I wanted so much. I already possessed that gift of cold reason and that sense of the practical which later on would help me to avoid many unpleasant experiences, and I knew that some trick of fortune could let me down so that I might be caught, just as I had surprised my parents. I felt that there was something wrong about all this, and I wanted to be very careful. Nevertheless, I was all aflame. The troublesome little place down there itched and tingled so that I clutched at my pillow, and it was only when I had made up my mind to go off to the country with my uncle so that I might have a chance to talk to Marguerite that I went to sleep.

I had no trouble in getting permission to leave, and my parents said I could spend a week away from home. My uncle's estate was a few leagues from town, and we set off after dinner. The whole day long I was as helpful and pleasant as possible, and Marguerite seemed to like my company. Of my two cousins, I didn't care much for the girl, and the boy was very shy. As he was the only young man I might see without arousing suspicion, I had at first thought of going to him about my problem. He could have explained all the enigmas which had been tormenting me since I had hidden myself in the alcove. I was very nice to him, even provocative, but he always avoided me. He was pale and thin, and his eyes seemed anxious and troubled, and he always seemed to find it upsetting and unpleasant if I touched him teasingly. I soon discovered the reason for his odd behavior, which had seemed all the more strange since all the young men whom I knew paid much court to us young ladies.

We arrived at my uncle's estate around eight o'clock on an evening that had turned hot and humid. Tired out by our journey, we hurried to our rooms to refresh ourselves. Afterwards we had tea, during which I, in a naive manner, arranged to sleep in the governess' room. I pretended that I would be afraid to sleep all alone in a strange room and everyone seemed to find it quite natural. I had got my own way and I was pleased, feeling certain that I could arrange everything else to suit my plans, too.

However, I was not to get to bed that night without having one more adventure. Even today it disgusts me to talk about it.

After tea, I had to go to the toilet outside, the two closets of which were arranged together, the doors side by side. The partition was made of rough planks, some of them separated by slight cracks. I was preparing to leave the place when I heard someone coming. The person went into the adjoining closet and bolted the door. Not wishing to leave before the other, I remained. In curiosity and without meaning any harm, I looked through one of the cracks and saw my cousin, who was occupied with something quite different from what I had thought. He was sitting with his legs outstretched, and he had his two hands where my father had often had his own while making love to my mother. He was feverishly trying to awaken his desires, and I saw that the thing soon began to take a quite different shape in his hands. He moistened it with saliva, and it began to swell and grow extraordinarily. His cold-looking eyes lit up gradually. After a few moments I saw him shudder, his lips twisted, and a jet of white foam suddenly shot out of his member, enigmatic for me, and ran down its length and over his hand which was resting now, still and tired.

This glimpse explained things to me, particularly all that my parents had said concerning a jet, filling me at the same time, however, with an overwhelming disgust. Even so, during the whole of this scene a growing nervousness had mixed itself with my curiosity, though the sight of the young man in his exhausted state filled me with repugnance. His eyes were clouded and troubled. My mother and father had seemed beautiful when they had finished, but my cousin seemed ugly, grotesque and filthy. I had understood quite well what Marguerite was doing because a young woman is always forced to give herself up to her feelings and pleasures in secret. Anyway, she had done it with enthusiasm, with vivacity and passion. My cousin, on the other hand, had acted in a mechanical and unromantic fashion, violently and like an animal. Whatever could prompt a strong, healthy young man to let himself go in such a miserable passion when he might have been satisfied so much more easily with any number of willing women and girls he had access to?

I felt as if I had been personally offended, even cheated of something. If he had come to me in a tactful way, I would probably have done for him what my mother had done for my father.

In the meantime, however, I had learned a lot of things and had drawn several conclusions. I no longer needed Marguerite's explanations to make the whole thing clear, but I just had to find out why people were so secretive about these matters. I wanted to know what danger lay in it, what exactly it was that was forbidden, and I wanted to try for myself these pleasures whose charms I had so recently seen. Night was falling and a heavy storm began to blow up. Just as we were going to bed, about ten o'clock, I heard the first clap of thunder. My little cousin, the girl, was sleeping in her parents' room, so that I was alone with Marguerite, and I watched very closely everything that she did. She bolted the door, opened her bag and put all her things into a cupboard, hiding the mysterious packet under a pile of linen with the book, which I had seen her reading. I made up my mind at once to make the most of my stay in the country, to have a good look at these objects and to study them carefully. Marguerite was going to have to confess everything to me without my having to threaten her with making public her secret joys. I was very proud to think that my ruse was going to take her by surprise, convince her, and seduce her, and that I was going to oblige her to tell me everything. My curiosity was still growing, but I don't know why I felt any particular pleasure in doing this.

The storm broke. The claps of thunder came one after the other without pause. I pretended that I was afraid, and Marguerite had hardly gotten into her bed when, at the first flash of lightning, I jumped out of my own and ran towards her, trembling all over. I begged her to let me get in with her, telling her that my mother always did so whenever there was a storm. She took me into her bed and stroked me to calm me down. I threw my arms around her and held her as closely as I could. At every flash I buried my face against her. Marguerite kissed me in a kindly fashion, but that was not what I wanted. I didn't quite know what to do to get more. The warmth of her body was all around me and made me feel very good. I hid my face between her breasts and a curious shudder ran all down my limbs. However, I didn't dare touch what I wanted. I was ready for anything and yet, now that my dreams were at the point of being realized, my courage had deserted me.

Suddenly I had an idea and complained of a pain between my thighs. I pretended ignorance of the cause and groaned a great deal. Marguerite touched me and I guided her hand this way and that. I assured her that it was less painful when I felt the warmth of her hand, and that the pain went away entirely when she massaged me. I said all this in such a forthright way that Marguerite didn't see through my subterfuge. In any case, her little touches were much too gentle and not at all passionate. I kissed her, pressed myself against her, held her tightly in my arms, imprisoned her hand and, little by little, became aware that her feelings were beginning to change.

Her hand entirely covered my important place, and her fingers carefully opened the young lips and felt for the entry which was unfortunately still closed. Marguerite was still much too hesitant. She was as scared as I was. These timid caresses, however, gave me an inexpressible pleasure, and I felt that desires were being awakened in her, too. But I was careful not to let her see that her caresses were giving me any more than a temporary relief from my supposed "pains." In actual fact, it was quite a different sensation to feel another person's hand in that place.

When her finger brushed the sensitive, pubescent little head a shudder raced through my body. I told her at once that the pain lay there and that I must have caught a chill because it hurt so much! She was obviously pleased to be able to relieve my pain with her fingers, and her caress now became exquisitely gentle. She slid her hand down, allowing it to linger longer and longer in the sensitive place, and finally tried to force it in. But that really did hurt, and when I quivered she withdrew quickly to where the pleasure was greatest. She was obviously becoming excited and more tender, and she held me more closely. She pulled up both our nightdresses as far as possible so that our bodies were touching now at their full lengths. I had got what I wanted. Although my expedient had not been very ingenious, she suddenly complained that she had a pain in the same place. She, too, had probably contracted a chill. I said that I would try to relieve it with my hand. This was quite natural since her hand was doing me so much good. She opened her thighs to make room for me and I was very pleased to see that my trick had succeeded so well. Nevertheless, I caressed the object of my desires clumsily and timidly. I did not want to give myself away. I was immediately aware of a very great difference.

Everything was much larger and more mature than in my case. My hand did not move—it contented itself with being there.

Finally, Marguerite could stand it no longer. She raised herself slightly, twisted her body about, and her thighs trembled and moved in a strange way. All at once she declared that her pain was much farther back than that. Obligingly, but without hurrying, I tried to relieve this unfortunate discomfort. With my forefinger I sought it as deeply as possible, deriving great pleasure from examining all the details of the admirable structure of her opening, but I was still so awkward and so inexperienced that Marguerite had to squirm about herself to reap the fruits of her dissimulation. And that was what she was doing. My hand was now playing the role which had been my father's when my mother had straddled him. Marguerite came closer, breathing heavily and trembling. She threw herself passionately upon my hand, and the full length of my fingers disappeared. At first, her inside was damp and sticky, but very soon it became burning and dry. By this time she was giving little inarticulate cries until my hand was suddenly drenched in a hot liquid, which I thought was the same as my cousin had ejaculated. Her excitement diminished at once and she relaxed beside me.

I had succeeded so far. Fortune had favored me and my trick had worked, but I wanted to carry our intimacy through to the end no matter what the cost. When Marguerite pulled herself together again she was very embarrassed. She didn't know how to explain her conduct to me and tried to hide her pleasure. My silence misled her. She thought that I had not realized what had happened, and I could tell she was thinking over what she could do, what she might tell me, so that the adventure would have no unpleasant consequences with regard to her position in my uncle's house. She wanted to hide from me the exact nature, the real cause of the "pain" she had felt. I didn't know what to do either. Should I pretend ignorance, or justify my behavior by admitting to her my curiosity? If I played the little innocent it would be easy for her to tell me any manner of story, which I would have to pretend to believe in order not to give myself away. Since I was more avid than anxious, I made up my mind to be sincere but to hide from her that it was by my calculations that this new situation had arisen. Marguerite seemed to be sorry she had allowed herself to give way to her passion, but I soothed her by telling her everything I had found out the day before. I begged her to be good enough to explain things to me fully, since her maturity, her movements, and the strange liquid that had flooded into my hand told me that she too had been initiated. I told her that I knew what games she played in secret, because I wanted to be sure that she wouldn't tell me lies. My naive inquisitiveness made her feel much better. She felt perfectly comfortable again, like an older woman giving good advice to someone young and inexperienced, and, as I told her in great detail everything of the day before—even about my mother's passionate conduct—she was no longer ashamed to tell me that apart from religion she knew of nothing more lovely in the world than sexual pleasure. And so she taught me everything; and if later on, you find some philosophy in these notes, I shall owe the first notions of it to dear Marguerite, who was so experienced and so eager to help me.

I learned about the exact conformation of both sexes, how union was accomplished, with what precious juices the natural human goals were attained—perpetuation of the human race and the greatest pleasure on earth—and why society draws a veil over these things and surrounds them in mystery. I also learned that in spite of all the dangers which surround them, the two sexes can still reach an almost complete satisfaction. She warned me of the unhappy consequences to which a young girl is exposed if she abandons herself completely. What my awkward hand had procured for her and what my cousin had done were among these almost complete satisfactions. Although she had tasted all the joys of love in the arms of a healthy young man, she was completely satisfied even when limiting herself to the pleasures which she could give herself: for she had had a child and she had known all the misfortunes of an unmarried mother. She showed me by the example of her own life that by keeping one's head and being prudent one could still have a lot of pleasure. The story of her life was very interesting and very instructive, and I shall make it the subject of my next letter. I had already guessed a lot of things for myself, but the new things she taught me were a source of continual surprise to me.

I found all of this very good, but it still wasn't the thing itself. I was burning to share and to know myself the sensations which, before my very eyes, had worked up persons of such varied types almost to the point of fainting. While Marguerite was talking, my hand had resumed its play in the place where she was so sensitive. I twisted the curls in her hairs and, when she moved more passionately, pressed and parted the smooth lips lovingly. I wanted to make her understand that my education would not be complete until I had had some experience myself. She told me about how she had given herself the first time to the young man who had made her a mother. She wanted me to understand the divine sensation that the male member had caused in penetrating. She spoke to me of the ecstasy, the full, shared delight she had experienced, and her words set me on fire. Her smooth rounded mound swelled and filled my hand, and her thighs tightened about me. The moment had come for me to remind her even more forcibly of these pleasures, and as she said, "You have to have experienced these things yourself to be able to understand them," I pushed my finger so deeply into the wide opening that she uttered a great sigh and immediately became silent. Feverishly, I rubbed the swollen lips which almost swallowed my hand, when I suddenly stopped and said to her, "If you want me to go on, you'll have to give me a taste of what is to come and of what you have so deliciously described." At once her fingers began to caress my little opening and I understood by the warmth of her kisses that my proposition gave her the keenest pleasure. She drew my finger out of her font, pushed in her own instead, moistened it, then came back to me and tried to make a way in. But it wasn't any good. In vain I opened my thighs and even the movement of my hips didn't help.

She said to me sadly, "This won't do, Pauline dear. Your body is still closed to love. Come sit on my face so that my mouth will be under your marvelous shell of love. I will see if my tongue can give you the pleasure which your virginity still makes impossible for you!"

My father had done this to my mother, so I didn't hesitate. I knelt down with her head between my thighs. She had hardly touched me when the tip of her tongue was already in the place that had hurt me so much when she had tried to push her finger in. But what a different feeling in comparison with everything I had tried up till then! As soon as her pointed, avid tongue touched me a new thrill, something I had never before experienced, spread over me. I no longer knew what was happening to me. We had thrown back the bedclothes and our bodies were one upon the other. I leaned over forward and putting my weight on my left hand played with the right in the depths of her "shell," as she had called it. These first sensations of pleasure, which I was still to feel even in my most mature years, already intoxicated me with an inexpressible joy. Her tongue sent searing waves of pleasure through my thighs. Marguerite teased the top, sucked at the bottom, breathed through every fold, kissed me all over passionately, moistened the interior with saliva, then came back to the entry where she lit in me a sweet and lingering fire. Something strange and wonderful was working up inside me. All of my juices were at the brink of discharge and I felt that, although I was so young, I was worthy of this pleasure. I wanted to return to her a hundredfold what she was giving to me.

Furiously, I drove in one, then two, then three fingers. My hand was seized by a cramp because of the awkward position in which I lay next to her, but we were beside ourselves with delight and we reached our goal together. I felt a great warm wave filling my inside while her sap flooded over my hand. I lost consciousness and fell upon the shuddering young woman, no longer aware of what was happening.

When I came to my senses again, I was lying beside Marguerite. She had pulled the covers over us and was holding me tenderly in her arms. Suddenly I realized that I had done something forbidden. My burning desire had been extinguished and my limbs ached. I felt a terrible itching in the places where Marguerite had so gently caressed me; the balm which flowed between my legs had no power to soothe me. I was conscious of having committed a crime and I burst into tears. Marguerite knew that in such cases there was nothing to be done with silly little girls like me. So she gathered me to her bosom and simply let me sob. Eventually I went to sleep.

This unique night was a turning point in my life. My whole being had changed and my parents noticed it upon my return. In astonishment they tried to find out what had happened. The relationship between Marguerite and myself had been of the strangest, too. By day we hardly looked at each other, while at night our intimacy was the wildest, our conversation the most obscene, and our pleasures the most lascivious. I swore to her that I would never let myself be seduced and never allow any man to pour into me his precious dangerous liquid. I wanted to find pleasure in everything that was without danger. A few days had sufficed to make me what I still am, and what you have so often admired.

I had noticed that everybody around me, even the most respectable people, had something to hide. Marguerite, who had told me everything, however, had never talked about that instrument which gave her as much joy as the hand or tongue and which contained the essential jet that I desired with all my soul.

She had never shown it to me, but it had occurred to me to steal the key to the cupboard where I knew it was locked up, and my curiosity gave me no peace. I didn't want to have to ask someone else about it—I wanted to find out for myself. For five days I couldn't get the key, but finally I managed to lift it and I seized the opportunity to satisfy my curiosity while Marguerite was giving my cousin a lesson. At last I had the thing in my hands. I turned it over and over and tried its elasticity. It was cold and hard. I tried to push the head of it in where, in Marguerite, it had disappeared entirely, but all in vain. It hurt me and I felt no pleasure. I couldn't get hold of any milk at that hour either, so I had to be content with warming the instrument in my hands. I had decided to open at last the way to those immense pleasures which others could feel and of which I had only had a foretaste. Marguerite had told me that even in a man's arms the first time was painful and that many women only found pleasure after many years of the most complete abandon to the man they loved. And so I tried again. I warmed the instrument between my breasts, and prepared my little font with a moist finger. I wanted to be able to receive the exigent guest. I noticed that the four nights I had passed with a mistress had wrought great changes in me. My finger penetrated halfway, but I could distinctly feel a little membrane stopping it. I had to pass it somehow. Marguerite had used oil, but

I had none, so I pressed the tip of the instrument in the scarcely visible opening and pushed and pressed until the strange head entered. That really hurt. The lips were burning and at length I felt something tear and a scalding liquid gushed out. Terrified, I saw it was blood. The instrument had only penetrated about a finger's length, but I was so excited that I put up with this pain and pressed harder and harder. I didn't feel the slightest pleasure and it hurt me a lot when I withdrew the cruel guest.

This experiment made me thoroughly miserable. I sponged the blood away carefully and washed myself several times. But all day long I felt the burning pain of the wound. Disillusioned, I put the instrument back in its hiding place. I was angry and annoyed with Marguerite for not having helped me. After so many pleasurable experiences, this one had been extremely nasty. I was afraid of the caresses Marguerite would give me that night and the discovery she was going to make, but as I had already told her lies it wasn't too difficult to do it once more.

After supper I told her a tale of having fallen off a ladder. I said that I had hurt my leg and that I had even been bleeding. In bed she examined me and, far from guessing what had happened, she confided to me that this fall had cost me my virginity. She wasn't at all sorry for me, but for my future husband, who would be cheated of my first fruits. I could not have cared less then than I did later! So as not to tire me, Marguerite sent me off to my own bed that night. I was glad of that. She smeared me with cold cream, and the next day I felt much better.

The last two nights that I spent in my uncle's

country home more than made up for this short privation. I knew then all the bliss that the entry of a warm, living, foreign body can produce in a woman. The sources of my pleasure flowed so freely that no desire remained unfulfilled. The completeness of the delight crushed me with an utter and delicious fatigue.

Although I experienced all of that at fourteen years of age, when my body was not yet mature, it has never had any bad effect on my health nor diminished my capacity for enjoyment. My cousin had taught me to beware of the prostration that follows excess, and thanks to my reasonable nature I never overdid it. I always calculated the possible results, and only once in my life did I ever forget myself enough to lose all of my self-control and my superiority. I had learned early that, according to the laws of society, you had to take your pleasure with a thousand precautions if you wanted to do it without coming to harm. Anybody who obstinately acts contrary to these laws eventually comes to grief, and he repents at leisure his hurried moments of enjoyment. It is true that I was lucky enough right at the beginning to fall into the hands of an experienced young woman. What would have become of me if, by any chance, there had been a young man among my acquaintances to take me artfully in hand? With my curiosity and my temperament, I should have been lost. And if I am not lost, it is thanks to the circumstances in which the matters of sex were revealed to me. It is exquisite as long as it is veiled, and yet it is the focal point of all human activity.

Before I begin my third letter, I note that a short time after my relations with Marguerite had finished, the signs of the complete development of my body began to show themselves for the first time.

IV

It is unusual for two women to have so much in common in their tastes, in their daily life, and even in their destiny as Marguerite and I. When she was warning me of the dangers of giving myself too fully to a man, and while she was enumerating all the unfortunate consequences that such a mistake could entail outside marriage, I should never have imagined that I, too, might have similar moments of forgetfulness. Before I go on, I want to relate briefly what I learned about Marguerite's life in the course of those few nights and in our subsequent relationship. Certain aberrations in my life will thus be explained rather better than I could otherwise account for them.

Marguerite was born in Lausanne and, after having been very well educated, she suddenly became an orphan at the age of seventeen. She was in possession of a small fortune and thought that her future was secure, but she had the bad luck to fall into the hands of an unscrupulous guardian. He wasn't unkind to her, but very quickly embezzled the little money she had.

Shortly after her parents' death she had gone into the service of a Viennese baroness who lived in a lovely villa at Morges on the banks of Lake of Geneva. Her work was chiefly as a lady's maid. The baroness was elegant and a woman of taste and spent hours at her toilet. For the first few days the baroness was very reserved, but she soon became more and more pleasant and began to ask Marguerite a lot of questions concerning, among other things, whether or not she had a lover. By the end of a fortnight, seeing that Marguerite was still innocent, the baroness became very familiar with her. One morning she asked Marguerite if she knew how to attend to a toilet more personal than anything she had ever done before. Marguerite said no with a blush, because she knew quite well what the baroness meant. She was told she would have to learn to do it if she were going to replace her former maid and if the baroness was to have any sort of confidence in her. And so the woman sat down on a sofa, stretched out her legs on the back of two chairs, parted her thighs, gave Marguerite a small, smooth and supple tortoise-shell comb and showed her how to comb the hairs.

For the first time, Marguerite saw uncovered what she had never before seen on another woman. In great embarrassment, she set about making this toilet—awkwardly at first, but gradually becoming more skillful by following the baroness' directions. The baroness was a very pretty woman, blonde, with a lovely complexion. She always washed herself very carefully, so this task was in no way repulsive. Marguerite described to me in loving detail the conformation of the baroness. She admitted that although feeling very embarrassed at first, she came to be very fond of this singular occupation, especially when she realized that the baroness was not indifferent to it. This lady sighed, rolled her hips and thighs, and the opening which at first had been closed widened slightly, the lips reddening, and the little bit that hung down like an earlobe trembling delicately. Of course, as soon as she was alone in her room, Marguerite tried out on herself this "personal toilet." Although inexperienced, she easily found out that nature had hidden in this part of a woman's body an inexhaustible source of pleasure, and she soon completed what the comb had begun.

Sharp-witted, like all young girls of her age, she realized that the baroness desired more than this simple prelude, but didn't want to admit it. She was soon to discover how easy complete accord is when desire is reciprocated. However, the situation remained the same for some weeks, each of them hoping that the other would make the first advance, each wishing to be the one seduced and the one who could accord her favors. Finally, one day, the comb yielded its place to the hand, and the baroness threw off all restraint and showed herself to be a sensual and very voluptuous woman who wanted to make the most of her beauty in spite of the bonds of marriage, for she had wed a man who had aroused desires in her that he had been unable to quench.

For the past two years he had held an important diplomatic post in Paris and, when he realized that his impotence had become complete, had sent his wife away to Lake of Geneva. The baroness was a very elegant woman, but lived the life of a recluse. Marguerite had noticed that a sort of majordomo, a bad-tempered old man, was there as a spy and dispatched accounts to Paris of everything he either saw or heard, so that the baroness was forced to abandon all hope of any masculine company. She was extremely prudent; she had to be for the sake of family interests. Nobody in the baroness' household or among those around her ever suspected the secret pleasures which Marguerite had discovered that day. After they had gotten over the first shame, the most dissolute scenes took place morning and evening between the young woman and the girl, between the mistress and the servant, while all day long the baroness never betrayed herself by the slightest familiarity. Marguerite used to get into the baroness' bed naked and she didn't need to tell me what they did together, since I had just experienced this myself. But in those days it had been Marguerite who had held the role that I played now. The baroness had been insatiable, always inventing new games, and knew how to draw ever-renewed delights through the contact of feminine bodies. Marguerite declared that this was the happiest and most voluptuous period of her life.

The baroness went to Geneva every week to shop and go visiting, the majordomo with her every time, and Marguerite was later permitted to accompany them. The same suite in one of the largest hotels was always reserved and it consisted of a drawing room, a bedroom, a little room for Marguerite, and next to it another for the majordomo. The doors of the rooms all opened into a corridor and the communication doors between rooms were all either locked or blocked by furniture.

After Marguerite had been to Geneva several times, she noticed that something odd was going on which the baroness was hiding from her. Her toilet was not being done in the same way anymore and there was no more feminine abandon either morning or evening. During the day the baroness seemed agitated, worried and nervous and her nightclothes and her bed revealed distinctly that she had not spent the night alone. The bed was always in the greatest disorder, chairs were pushed over, and the toilet linen showed even more significant signs. Marguerite watched her with a kind of jealousy. She inspected every letter, kept watch for every visitor and every messenger boy, but could not discover a thing. However, on every trip that they made she became more and more convinced that the baroness was not spending her nights alone. In vain she listened outside the doors. The baroness locked not only the door into the corridor but the one leading from the drawing room to the bedroom as well. It was impossible to listen outside the corridor door for long because travelers and the hotel servants were always passing. Marguerite spent whole nights at her half-opened door to see if anyone went in or out of the baroness' room.

This watching and spying lasted over a period of several months until, one night, a fire broke out near the hotel. The hotel manager had all the guests awakened to warn them of the danger. Marguerite dashed to the baroness' room, where her terrified mistress opened the door to her. The glow from the fire shone through the window. The baroness was so frightened she could hardly speak and seemed to have lost her head completely. Marguerite shot a glance around the room and at last discovered what she had wanted to know. The wardrobe which stood in front of the door to the next room had been moved away from the wall. Someone could have easily passed behind it. A man's coat lay on the chair by the bed and on the bedside table lay a man's watch with some charms attached to the chain. There was no longer any possible doubt. The baroness realized that Marguerite had noticed the objects but was too upset to make any excuses. Marguerite packed up all the baroness' belongings so that they could leave if it became necessary and, in doing so, noticed a little bladder which seemed to have been used. When the baroness had become a little calmer she tried to hide the object in her handkerchief. The fire, in the meantime, was soon brought under control and this incident brought no change in their relationship.

The next morning, before they left Geneva, Marguerite learned from the hotel servants that a young Russian count occupied the room next to the baroness. It so happened that the rooms were situated at a turn in the corridor so that the count could go in and out without passing the baroness' suite if he used the staircase at the other wing of the hotel. Everything became clear to Marguerite now. The baroness must have slept with him many times, and Marguerite was offended that this had been hidden from her. On the way back to Morges the baroness surreptitiously threw away her handkerchief and once they had arrived life went on as usual. The baroness didn't know whether or not she ought to admit everything to Marguerite, although she knew that the girl was perfectly aware of all that had happened.

On their next visit to Geneva, Marguerite spent all of her spare time in the corridor, where she met the young count several times. He was young, handsome and elegant, and the second time he encountered her he turned around. The third time he spoke. When he learned that she was the maid of a lady living in the hotel—Marguerite was careful not to mention her mistress' name—he waited no longer and invited her into his room. For no reason other than curiosity—at least that is what she told me several times—she followed him. Once inside he kissed her, stroked her breasts and, in spite of her struggles, found to his satisfaction that she was as young and well built as he had hoped. While the young man's hands amused themselves in this most pleasant way, Marguerite glanced quickly about the room. She saw which door led to the baroness' room and quickly worked out her plan. The count wanted to get right down to business, but met irritated resistance. He had to be content with Marguerite's promise to come that night when her mistress was asleep.

She said that she didn't want to come until well after midnight when the corridor would be dark. He thought it over for a few seconds, while Marguerite laughed inwardly at his predicament. The attraction of a new conquest was stronger than his scruples, however, so they arranged to meet at one o'clock. She persuaded him to give her the key to his room so she could enter quickly at an opportune moment. Her victory had been won, and she worked out her plans to the smallest detail.

The baroness dismissed Marguerite at ten o'clock, carefully locking the door behind her, but instead of going back to her own room Marguerite listened outside the baroness' door. After a minute or two she heard her humming a tune—something she never did as a rule. Then she heard a slight tapping on the wall. Marguerite heard the wardrobe being moved and the inside door opening. She knew that the count would be in the baroness' room, so she hurried to his chamber and slipped in silently, making sure that no one saw her. A ray of light showed through the half-open door between the two chambers, and she could easily see what was happening in the baroness' room. The lady was lying back upon her bed in the arms of the count, who was covering her neck, her mouth and her bosom with burning kisses, while his hands strayed between her thighs. The baroness was a beautiful woman, but it was not on her charms that Marguerite's eyes lingered. Full of curiosity, she stared at the man who was as yet a stranger to her. The count undressed rapidly, showing himself as well built as he was handsome, and at that moment Marguerite saw the organs of a man for the first time. What was her embarrassment to see the baroness then enclose the shining enemy, which she had just been stroking and kissing, in a little bladder which she removed from a box on the bedside table. This whitish object had a tiny red cord attached to one end of it and had been invented by an English doctor named Condom. Having finished this strange toilet, she smeared the object of her desires with perfumed oil, then lay back on the bed while the count knelt between her thighs so that it would be more easy to enter. Suddenly, with one quick motion, he made his entry and the two bodies locked in a passionate embrace. However, Marguerite didn't see as much as I had from my alcove because the baroness pulled the bedclothes over them. She could only see their two heads, mouth to mouth, drinking in kisses. Then the count sighed deeply and slumped down on the baroness' bosom, exhausted. They lay there locked together for a full quarter of an hour, during which time the baroness never relaxed her embrace. Marguerite confessed to me that she couldn't help calming with her hand the tremendous itching of her inside, but she also confessed that after what she had seen she desired another, fuller satisfaction.

Marguerite also explained to me the object and use of the precautionary measure which she had seen and which had averted such misery and shame in the world. She immediately understood the use of it when she saw the baroness withdraw the red cord hanging between her thighs, and remove the bladder from her body to lay it upon the bedside table. This, then, was the shield of protection which allowed unmarried women, widows, and those women afflicted with tired husbands to give themselves unfearfully to the pleasures and delights of love.

Marguerite had seen enough. She could now force the baroness to confess. Though she was all aflame, she put off for that night getting to know the count any better, for she wanted to be certain that he would use this prophylactic. She didn't want to run any more risk than necessary, and she mentioned to me, too, that she would have found it unpleasant to play second fiddle to the baroness. Prudently, she went back to her room and banged the door behind her. She was delighted, and now the count might wait for her in vain the rest of the night.

She was in complete mastery of the situation. She wanted to take part in these games; she wanted to be revenged on the baroness, who would not make her a confidante. She reflected all night on how she could turn her advantage to good account. You will be amazed to learn how

Marguerite conceived her plan and with what consequence she applied it. Astuteness is an essential quality of the womanly nature, and I have seen some admirable examples of it, for everything connected with the divine pleasure of a woman's natural cunning and dissimulation are sharpened to an incredible degree. The most stupid becomes inventive under the influence of capriciousness, envy or love. The means employed by women and girls to reach their aims are endless.

Before the baroness awoke, Marguerite went and knocked on the count's door. He came to open it in his dressing gown, thinking it was a servant, and was amazed to see Marguerite, whom he had vainly awaited since after midnight. He reproached her, wanted to draw her into his bed and make up for lost time at once, but soon changed his manner when she began to upbraid him instead. She told him she had come a little before the appointed hour and had seen what had been going on. She said that she could get a large reward from the baroness' husband if she were to tell him about it. She added, however, that she would not do such a thing on condition of being allowed to take part in their games with the same guaranty of safety. She would even help the baroness in her pleasures and assist them in their affair.

The count was too surprised to speak for several moments. He finally recovered enough to promise to do anything provided she kept quiet, for if any talk of his affair with the baroness should get abroad, both of their families would be exposed to the greatest danger. She explained her whole plan to him and insisted that he implement it before the baroness' departure, which was planned for that same morning. Surprised to find the young woman, so farsighted and pleased to see his love affair so pleasantly involved, the count was in complete agreement. And when Marguerite allowed him to make free with her, he was even more surprised to find her a virgin. He could not have hoped to find a sweeter companion in pleasure. He even wanted to prove his enthusiasm for her there and then, but Marguerite opposed him energetically, only serving to heighten his passion. He could hardly wait for the moment to carry out their plan. Marguerite had tasted enough in this one visit not to want to leave the full possession of so charming a young man to the baroness alone. They had decided upon the details of what was to come an hour later, and Marguerite accorded the handsome count a number of delightful things—everything, in fact, except what he wanted most of all. She left the room, finally, of a young man feverish with desire.

The baroness rang at seven o'clock, unlocked her door, and got back into bed. Marguerite put everything in order, prepared the luggage, and last of all served breakfast. All was ready. In his room, the count was waiting for the agreed signal. At length Marguerite went into the drawing room, banging the door. This was the sign. The count threw open his door, pushed back the wardrobe, and flung himself on the terrified baroness, covering her with kisses. She was too frightened to utter a word, and could only point to the door of the drawing room in which Marguerite was noisily closing up some trunks. The count pretended to push the bolt, then he begged the baroness to grant him, one last time, her supreme favor. He said she had been so seductive the previous night that he was afraid that if she refused him, he might become ill. He assured her that he was already provided with the safety device and that she had nothing to fear. The baroness, probably to get rid of the intruder as quickly as possible, opened her legs to receive this hot-blooded young man. Suddenly, the count heaved a great sigh and Marguerite, who had been listening outside the door, marched in. Simulating utter amazement at what she saw before her, she dropped what she was carrying and stared wide-eyed at the bed and the baroness who, with legs wide apart, was visibly though fearfully awaiting the supreme moment, for all was at stake— honor and fortune. The count swore an incomprehensible Russian oath and hurled himself at Marguerite. In a towering rage he cried, "We are lost if I don't kill this *traitresse* and silence her forever! We dare not let her leave this room."

Marguerite made as if to run away, but the count blocked the doorway. He gave her the terrible look of a man about to strangle her, while the baroness watched the scene more dead than alive. Suddenly, as if he had just thought of it, the count stopped and cried, "But wait! There is a better way to gain this girl's silence! We must make her our accomplice. Forgive me, my dear baroness, I am only doing this for you."

As he spoke, he grabbed Marguerite, who pretended to be frightened out of her wits, flung her down on the bed beside the still naked and trembling baroness, picked up her skirts, and threw himself violently between her legs. Marguerite twisted about, pretending to try to escape his grasp, although in reality she was offering herself more and more. She would not let him in until she was sure that she had nothing to fear. However, he was still wearing the strange mask which he had donned for the baroness, and when she saw it she opened the way for him, pretending to give in to his violence. She moaned faintly, begging the baroness to help her, to save her from the rage of this madman. Inwardly, she was entirely given up to the sensations which flooded her bosom. She was secretly delighted with this trick she was playing the baroness on her own bed, beside her own naked form, and to be receiving from such a fine man what should have been the baroness' by right. In spite of his apparent violence, the count handled her with tenderness and slowly provoked the flow of those most precious liquids, which could fill her now without danger. Not only was the baroness present, but she also had to calm the weeping Marguerite and beg her not to shout so loudly. Beside all that, as the crisis approached, the count said to her, "Dear baroness, if you don't help me to master this girl, we are lost. We can only rely on her if I manage to rape her." And the baroness dragged Marguerite's thighs roughly apart, while the count penetrated to the root. Marguerite struggled to close her legs, fighting against the baroness. This exertion provoked sudden spasms and starts, which increased the pleasure and caused an immediate and reciprocal flow of the sources of pleasure. Marguerite seemed to have passed out, but she listened to and observed everything.

The count had dressed quickly. He went down on his knees before the baroness, begged her to calm herself, and to forgive him for having used such a means. He assured her that it was the only way to remove the danger, and he made it clear that they had won a very sure confidante in Marguerite and that their love affair would be in no danger whatsoever. He added, moreover, that if they gave her some money she would become more closely attached to them. He pretended to have made an enormous sacrifice for the baroness in lowering himself to a chambermaid. Finally, he besought the baroness to use every means in her power to console and win Marguerite when she got over her fainting fit. Marguerite made a little movement as if she were about to wake up, and the baroness, perceiving the little red cord hanging there, pulled it out quickly and hid it among the bedclothes. What a triumph for Marguerite! The baroness had personally rendered her such a service!

Having arranged their next meeting, the count went back to his own room, leaving the two women alone. The baroness, utterly deceived and very worried, attempted to amuse Marguerite by telling her about her affair with the count, but Marguerite seemed inconsolable. The baroness also told her about the life she had led with her husband and promised to take care of her in the future if she would only help her and forgive her for the count's violence. Eventually Marguerite stopped complaining about the suffering she had endured and promised the baroness that since she had, in spite of herself, found out about the secret she would help to arrange their meetings.

All said and done, a very strange liaison grew up between these three people. The count had no idea of the secret intimacy between the two women. He had had enormous pleasure with Marguerite's beautiful young body and he liked her hardly-trodden pathway. He preferred it, in fact, to that well-worn avenue of the baroness and when they were alone he gave her the most significant proof of his love and his favor. In the baroness' presence, Marguerite hardly paid any attention to the count. She declared that she only took part in their revels to please the baroness who, for her part, had no suspicion of what was going on between her lover and her chambermaid. She showered Marguerite with presents and made her her confidante in all things. On their next trip to Geneva, Marguerite was present every time the count came to the baroness' room in the evening, but she had already been to his to gather the first fruits of his strength. Thus the baroness was becoming the recipient of nothing but leftovers.

Marguerite never tired of telling me of all the pleasures that such an agreement between three persons can bring. Especially when some little romance, some slight intrigue, involves itself also. She told me that she was always passive so as not to arouse the baroness' suspicions, but Marguerite and the count knew exactly where they stood. The young Russian was as tender as he was passionate. He adored her because he was the first to ascend to her virginal throne. However, he wanted to persuade Marguerite to try without the condom and discover what it was like to feel, at the decisive moment, a flow of life-force spreading through the vagina. He also told her that the mixing of these precious saps gave off a delightful perfume, and that it was like a foretaste of heavenly bliss. He also promised her that he would take care of her if she should conceive and give birth to a child. But Marguerite said no emphatically. She said that it was enough to feel the impetuous flood of her own body and that she didn't want any of his dampness or his balsamlike fecundity.

After they had taken their pleasure together, the revels went on again during the evenings in the baroness' room and lasted until late at night. From their first experience as a trio, the baroness was plainly delighted, for the count was very inventive. They amused themselves in all sorts of ways. Marguerite lay down on the baroness, the center of her pleasure on the mount's mouth, while he drove his scepter into the baroness from beneath, his tongue in Marguerite's font, while the baroness licked her round little breasts. The count was inexhaustible in many ways, increasing and provoking the greatest pleasure by long preliminaries in the most diverse fashions. The baroness would lie down on the bed in such a way that the count would be standing before her or leaning over her, while Marguerite, sitting on a stool, had her eyes just at the level of the acting parts. She would put her hands there, sometimes playing with the so well filled font of the baroness, sometimes with the scepter and the two balls of the aggressor. With her fingers she would open the great lips and the velvety flesh, which closed with its thousand folds even more vigorously around the host, drawing it in. Then she would bring one hand down on the embraced tip, which could hardly get out, while with her other hand she held the lance and squeezed it so tightly that it could no longer enter.

When she would open her hand, the member would disappear at once into the depths. She would also stroke the recipient of this admirable liquor, exciting every fiber to relax. The baroness' dazzlingly white thighs, which passed beneath the hemispheres of alabaster, round and swollen, the blonde hair of the temple, the brilliant red of the priest, who was to sacrifice there, the splendid limbs of the man who was then in his prime, his black hairs mingled with the blonde ones—and to take part in this spectacle, to savor it with the eyes from so close, to share in spirit the pleasures of the other two—so many delights all at once! Marguerite grew heated at the memory of these admirable things, and as her hand grew more and more licentious in the downy warmth of the bed, I felt that these images inflamed her.

Indeed the situation of these three persons was highly unusual. In spite of their great intimacy there still existed a reciprocal distrust. As I have already told you, such images delight my imagination, but my reason warns me not to imitate them. Such subtleties are followed by great fatigue, and difficulties always arise when a secret is known to more than two people. As the young count could satisfy all his caprices, he soon tired of this liaison. He grew colder and colder, probably tired out by the exigencies of the two women. In short, he left Geneva suddenly after a cold farewell and the baroness, wanting to get rid of Marguerite, soon found an opportunity. Marguerite had received more than three thousand francs from the count and the baroness. Unfortunately, she had handed over this money to her guardian, so she went to live with a friend who had once been a governess. She took lessons because she intended to go to Russia as a governess, as many Swiss women did.

However, the change in her situation was too sudden. She wasn't happy in her friend's home and her studies bored her. In the baroness' house she had had everything to make her happy. She had even had the chance to taste pleasures ordinarily forbidden to most women and practically all girls. She was spoiled and her body had grown to need certain things. She missed the count's beautiful young figure and the baroness' intimate caresses.

During all of the first months away, her nights were restless and her dreams troubled. The effect of her hand was negligible and she found no opportunity of getting to know anyone reliable. She would have been quite happy to give herself to anybody on condition that she would have had nothing to fear. She did not dare to propose to any other man, of course. what she had proposed to the count in rather special circumstances. A young girl never admits these things because it would lower her in men's eyes, so she spent a very lonely year among her books. Something had been awakened in her that she could not satisfy, and which broke out tyrannically at night in her dreams.

Finally, in a thermal bathing house she met a young girl with whom she soon had relations as intimate as those she had had with the baroness. All sorts of games, curious conversations, the teaching of forbidden things and daring experiencies procured for them deep and thrilling delights. They soon admitted other companions to their revels, each one pretending to know nothing, each allowing herself to be taught things which they had practiced in secret.

Marguerite was insatiable. These secret meetings, these clandestine amusements sharpened her desire. One day she met the brother of one of her new friends. He was a pleasant, well-mannered young man and she saw at once that he liked her. He approached her with the emotion and awkwardness of an adolescent who feels himself attracted for the first time to a woman. Marguerite had great difficulty in hiding her passion. She would willingly have satisfied his last desire, which he did not yet know about, but she didn't know how to explain about her insistence on security measures. Charles had been brought up in the country and was entirely ignorant of these things, and his words and actions were simple and honest. Marguerite, face to face at last with love, thought she knew everything, and thought she was mistress of her heart. But all her principles evaporated in the heat of the first kiss. She was defenseless before the hesitating caresses of her beloved. He was so awkward that she had to lead him without appearing to do so. Marguerite was highly amused to see the commendable efforts that he made to reach a goal, the existence of which he scarcely suspected. She felt so superior to him that she believed that she would be able to keep her head at the fatal moment, for her young sweetheart was already in raptures at the slightest touch. She thought that she could stop him from pouring out the semen inside her and she let him enter. What she didn't realize was that her every fiber and every nerve was awaiting this union. She did not realize the weakness of a woman in the arms of the man she loves when all his virile strength warms her inwardly, and makes her forget all safeguards, all principles, until suddenly there was the electrifying discharge of a burning flow which filled her entirely.

So there it was. She hoped that nothing had happened in this single embrace, but it was in vain that she forbade him to approach her. When her periods failed to appear it was obvious that misfortune had been accomplished. She was dishonored and her future was ruined. And so she accorded him all the rights of a husband. For three months they tasted all the joys of earthly happiness, until the blows of cruel destiny fell upon her. Her guardian went bankrupt and fled to America carrying off her money, and her lover fell ill and died. Covered with shame, she was chased from the house. She sought refuge in a poor village where she lost her child after two years of privation and suffering. Eventually she came to Germany and found this post as governess in my uncle's house.

How often she warned me of the danger of such abandon. Marguerite, with simplicity and frankness, had taught me everything, yet she concealed from me the instrument which brought her souvenirs to life again.

V

Few young girls have learned in so short a time, and especially after taking so few risks, all that concerns the most important act in a woman's life as I happened to learn it, thanks to Marguerite's story. Up until then I had known no more (and probably no less) than most young girls of my age, although I was by nature more sensual than girls or young women usually are.

Men make the mistake of thinking that the female sex is naturally as sensual as their own, and they think wrongly that all women are easy. Married men, who are always complaining, know quite well that this is not true.

At first, I didn't want to believe it either; I thought that it was all deceit and dissimulation when I found in a woman coldness, indifference, and disgust for the very things which excite me. After hearing this, you will probably wonder why so many young girls let themselves be seduced if nothing within them draws them towards sexual relations, and if their sexuality and their sense of pleasure are not as violent as that of men. Although I know that unfortunately there is a lot of truth in this observation, I cannot account for it. Yet my observations and my personal experiences have convinced me more and more that conscious sensuality is not as highly developed in a woman as in a man. It is awakened and provoked gradually and it is usually only between the ages of thirty and forty years that it is as demanding in a woman as in a man. I don't understand why so many women allow themselves to be so easily seduced, for their later misfortune, when they are by no means in complete accord with the man who does it. I have never managed to find any explanation for this contradiction.

Everything is against a man when he is trying to persuade one of these innocent young girls to give herself completely. The physical pain of the first contact is so great that it serves as a warning, making one think twice about continuing further down the pathway of desire. The fear of inevitable consequences holds them back also, for few young girls are silly enough not to realize what they are risking. Statues, pictures, the sight of the mating of animals, books they are bound to come across, boarding school chatter, everything brings as much instruction, even to the most naive, as if she had the thousand eyes of Argus. Yes—and yet there is something that I must admit to you, for I find no other explanation for it. Very often it is curiosity and the need to give themselves entirely to the men they love which impels them. But how many give themselves without love? How many weep and sob without defending themselves? This is one of the most surprising mysteries of nature, and it is the most characteristic example of the strength and power of attraction which she imposes even on the most uncommunicative of temperaments.

From the lion to the merest of domestic animals, the entire cat species mates in pain and gives birth in pleasure (it is just the contrary to what happens in every other living creature) and yet the female always offers herself to the pain of the mating. Who can shed light on this problem? How many young girls have declared to me in tears that they didn't know how it had ever happened. "He asked me so sweetly." "It was so warm, so lovely." "I was so ashamed." All of these phrases explain nothing. It seems then very strange that I, who have such an ardent nature (I don't mind telling you this, for you are not going to take advantage of it) should have a will strong enough to have avoided these dangers for a very long time. I can only recount my personal feelings and thoughts when the fatal hour came to me in my turn, but I shall do this in all sincerity by telling you later of that period of my life. In the meantime, none of the explanations given suffices to solve this most ancient of enigmas, and it probably never will be solved. It is not by mere chance that the history of the world begins with Eve's curiosity and the enjoying of the forbidden fruit. The sages who placed this myth at the beginning of the story of the human race knew that it was, in fact, the center, the cornerstone, the mystery of the whole world's story, and they were right—except in one thing: the enjoyment of the forbidden fruit did not close the gates to paradise—it opened them.

You can well imagine that I did not make all of these observations when I returned, so completely changed, to my parents' house. They are fruits of my subsequent experiences. I was only a child when I found myself in the alcove of my mother's bedroom, and I returned from my uncle's home still only a young girl, although I was no longer in my original, unsullied state. I was different and the world around me seemed to have changed. A veil had fallen from before my eyes and I saw everything, people and things, in a different light. I understood things which I had never even noticed before. Chance had taught me everything, but it had also made me wary of wasting my precious joys. My cousin had made me afraid of excesses. His pale face, his lusterless eyes, the whole aspect of this depraved young man had shown me the fate of those who indulge themselves too violently in secret pleasures. I have never been afraid of having recourse to them, but I have never done it at the cost of my health and gaiety. Yes, if I had been a man, I should probably never have practised them, for men have not the same excuse for these secret games as girls, women and widows. They are not so restricted or bound as women, who dare not make a sign, exchange a glance, or openly taste of the things of love without risking their honor and immediately becoming the prey of evil tongues. We always have to simulate indifference; even when we would like to act openly we have to do it in secret. And it makes us unhappy not to be able to admit that we are not indifferent.

However, a man is not obliged to observe a thousand conventions. For him there is only pleasures and joy, and it is we who bear all the pain. Why then does he lose in secret in his cold hand that which he can always find so many opportunities to put to much better use? As I was saying over-indulgence, which is always dangerous, is particularly so in that which concerns love, and this knowledge, acquired by chance, has so far kept me gay, joyful and sensual. I returned to my parents' house richer in the knowledge that there are two kinds of morals in the world: official, which uphold the laws of the bourgeois society and which no one may infringe with impunity, and natural morals, between the two sexes, of which the mainspring is pleasure.

Of course, I knew nothing of these ethics, and barely guessed at them—by instinct probably—and I should never have been able to systematize them or put them into words. However, I have often pondered this question since then and the double nature of it has always been perfectly apparent to me. What is morally acceptable in Mohammedan countries, for example, may be immoral in Christian lands. The morals of antiquity are equally different from the morals of the Middle Ages, and what was permissible in the Middle Ages often offends our feelings now. The law of nature is the most intimate union between man and woman; the form in which this union is accomplished depends upon the climate, on religious convictions, and upon the social order. No one can transgress with impunity these laws which are imposed upon him, and the restraint which the moral laws of a country exercise upon all of its people can stimulate their sensual pleasures by making them more secretive and more personal.

My parents observed, in exemplary fashion, the exterior forms demanded by law and custom, and for that reason they were doubly happy in their hours of pleasure. If I had not seen this myself I would never have believed it. Thus am I right in never trusting to appearances in matters such as these. The flashing eye, the coquettish manner, and the so-called loose conduct of certain women are just as misleading. I know by experience that women who seem to promise a lot are, in fact, those who are coldest and most insensitive—even when they keep their promises. "Still waters run deepest." The truth of this proverb is most clearly demonstrated by the conduct of women. We are capable of pretense even at the moment of fainting. I have seen this, not only in the case of my revered mother, but in others and even in myself. It is very uncomfortable for a woman to show that she feels pleasure herself in the act of love. We give pleasure and we let it be known that it is that which makes us happy, but something inexplicable forbids us to admit or to show to what extent we enjoy these delights. I believe that there is no other reason for this than the vague desire not to accord to the man we love any other rights than those which he already has upon us, and not to allow him to increase his power over us.

By nature a man must battle and vanquish these difficulties, attaining new and greater heights each time. Complete satisfaction makes a man indifferent, lazy and self-satisfied, and it would mean the attaining of this perfection if a woman admitted or gave any external sign of her pleasure. A man must always have something to fight for and win; a woman, too, must always have something to accord, even when she has already granted her supreme favors, so that when the physical victory is already won there should still remain a mental and emotional victory ahead. That is not mere calculation on our part. It is instinct. How often have I observed animals, the admitted masters of men in all the ways of nature, in their love play. The female defends herself, retreats, finally runs; the male pursues, forces and overpowers. When the male has finally achieved his goal, reduced every defense, he is through and he leaves. Then it is up to the female to chase him, demanding help, protection and subsistence. Except in a few rare species of animal, the female gives no sign of feeling pleasure, but she can never conceal her desire. She takes the male by surprise, excites him and seduces him. When he is at last on fire he meets with refusal and resistance and must fight. I believe that by these stratagems nature intended to create the greatest possible excitement and the most complete draining of the precious animal saps, the fusion of which assures the perpetuation of the species. They distill, vaporize and relax the nerve centers, making the union more complete. This is why the children born of a love combat are stronger than the children born of a dull, boring marriage, those "conceived between waking and sleeping," as Shakespeare has said. The provocation and refusal are, then, the result of natural laws just as are the desire of the man to obtain a complete submission and the woman's instinctive refusal of it. When the woman complains of her husband's coldness, it is because she has been too sincere at the moment of greatest pleasure and because she has not left a single desire unsatisfied in the man.

My mother had concealed the pleasure which she found in the mirror. Marguerite had not shown me her instrument. And yet I knew that these two women were sensual to the extreme. I have not forgotten this lesson as you will see.

All of these things kept my imagination busy in the most agreeable way. However, at this point I actually knew nothing of these theoretical things except for the experience I had had in connection with my cousin. I had seen two well-behaved, virtuous beings throw themselves into the joys of union, tasting the delights of complete and reciprocal possession. With Marguerite some desire had always remained unsatisfied, and now I felt that for myself there was something more complete to come. I still knew nothing really about the physical and mechanical side of animal pleasure, and even in my cousin's secret sensuality there remained a touch of mystery. Had I any idea what motivated him? Did I know all human passions? What offended me was, in fact, chiefly his indifference with regard to myself, a fresh young girl who came to offer herself to him. Actually, Marguerite and I were as guilty as he. If Marguerite had not put me on my guard I should have fallen into excess because of my curiosity and inexperience.

I should, perhaps have ruined my health like millions of anemic, young, haggard-eyed women who take the opportunity which every moment of solitude offers to jealously taste that which both manners and morals forbid. You can well imagine that after so many experiences I watched people and things through different eyes. Everywhere I saw secrets and dissimulation and suspected intrigues among all those around me. Usually I was wrong, as I had to admit later. I was all eyes and all ears, trying to find out what people were hiding from me and what people had hidden from me up until then. I would have liked to have caught my parents again, and I made a thousand plans to do so, but I was too frightened to execute them. Frankly, I was too ashamed to stoop so low, and I am glad now that I didn't. To spy upon them voluntarily would have been sacrilegious. And why sully the peace and joy of two good people? I did not need to reproach myself for having discovered them by accident or for having discovered Marguerite's lasciviousness.

Everything was still poetry to me, but I was soon to discover prose. I have already told you that soon after my return home I became a young woman. I noticed the first signs of my maturity with terror, and I wanted to hide them from my mother, for I thought the blood was a result of my misbehavior with Marguerite. Nevertheless, my linen betrayed me, and my mother talked to me for the first time about matters of this sort. She told me just enough to give me a general idea, but did not suspect that her own example had been a far better education. Shortly after this, I was confirmed (I was sixteen years old) and my parents took me with them into society. I was noticed, particularly because my voice was developing and my singing began to blossom. Every time I sang in public people would say from every side, "You ought to dedicate yourself to the theatre and become another Catalini, another Sonntag!"

Things which you hear repeatedly finally imprint themselves upon your mind and, although my father would at first have nothing to do with it, I found an ally in my mother. Eventually, it was decided that I should become a singer and all my studies were aimed in this direction. At the age of sixteen I enjoyed more liberty than most young girls. A distant relation, old, ugly and timid, was to accompany me to Vienna where I was to have my voice trained by a famous professor. My father had done all that his fortune would permit, and you know how grateful I am to him. Before my departure, I saw Marguerite several times more. She was my friend, my confidant and my mistress in those things in which a master is more usual. I was amazed to find out that she was having a love affair with my cousin, and when I made a remark to her about it she seemed very embarrassed. I had told her some time before what I had seen and she had been tempted by the idea of leading him away from his vice. She told me that my story had excited her imagination and that she had found an opportunity to overcome his horror of women. She pretended that she was ashamed of having seduced him. My cousin was ten years younger than she, but she assured me that she did not grant him any more than she had me. A burnt child fears the fire, and she remembered with regret the suffering she had endured for her beloved Charles. I have never been able to find out whether or not she told me the truth.

I noticed with pleasure that my cousin looked much better and that he no longer avoided girls. He even looked at me sometimes with an odd expression in his eyes. However, I didn't want Marguerite's help at all, and I contented myself with just teasing him. If I had not previously surprised him I believe that I would have had a very sweet relationship with my cousin, for we had the opportunity to see each other freely, and that is an essential condition for the pastimes of love. I was also terribly afraid of the ghastly consequences. Marguerite had talked to me about all this, so I made my first steps into the world well-armed and much more knowing than most young girls, a fact that has always proven useful to me, for I have always known exactly what was going on and what I was risking. People thought me cold and virtuous, when I was simply informed and prudent. If one wanted to analyze the so-called virtue of many women, one would come to some edifying conclusions. I have made it a duty to be sincere with you, but I believe that nearly all women have difficulty in being sincere, for deceit and pretense are part of our nature. If we could magically avoid the fatal consequences there would be no more virtuous women. Everyone would try out of sheer curiosity, knowing nothing unhappy would come of it.

Before leaving my father's house and setting out on the thorny and joyful path of that of an actress, I had the chance to discover another side to the ageless story. My parents possessed, besides our town house, a farm with cows, a barnyard and a big orchard. The chickens and the pigeons were my domain and I was responsible for feeding them. The chicken house was next to the barn and was separated only by a partition of planks from the part where the hay was piled up. I was there one morning when the coachman, who had only been in our service for two weeks, came through the cow shed pushing the servant girl into the barn. She was grinning, ugly, dirty and totally disgusting. She hardly struggled at all and abandoned herself as soon as he pushed her into the hay. I was standing behind the partition and watched them through a knothole.

I wish I had never seen them because it is impossible to imagine an uglier contrast to anything I had thus far known. With no tenderness whatsoever and without the least lingering over preliminary fondlings, he pulled up the girl's skirts, mauled her breasts and the object of his vile desires, then threw himself upon her and did everything that my father had done to my mother. He was easily as brutal as my father had been tender and was so much like an animal that I wanted to turn my eyes away. I still don't know why I did not. The words they exchanged were even more sickening, and they had vile expressions for everything which I had not yet heard mentioned by name. Finally a quick spasm brought the torrent of filth to an end, leaving me mentally exhausted from watching so disgusting a spectacle. However, I was afraid of revealing my presence so I had to remain for the girl's maneuvers as she attempted to excite the coachman again by the most unwomanly gestures and words. He seemed to have had enough, however, and was in no hurry to respond once more to her desires. Finally she compelled him to do so, and this time it lasted much longer than the first. She followed every thrust with exclamations that betrayed her pleasure, but were none the less disgusting for it.

Revolting as it had been, I was the richer for this new experience. In her ugliness this girl had shown me the seamier side of what my imagination had adorned with the beauties of the most sublime poetry. What a difference between the assuaging of their brutal desires and the tender and intimate union of two well-bred people! What is there left of this thing if you take away from it tenderness, fear and spirituality! There could be no question of love between them, not even foundness. He had been with us for only two weeks and what I had just seen was probably not their first performance. She had yielded to the new arrival the rights of his predecessor and did not find it in the least unusual. But how did she manage to avoid the consequences of her indulgences? I knew that the coachman was not the only one to enjoy the favors of this wench, and her cries showed that she absorbed everything to the last drop. She had obviously had no idea of taking precautionary measures. Here was food for thought. Of course, it is true that a farm servant does not need to worry much about losing her reputation even if she does bring into the world one of those miserable little wretches that bear the burden of their parents' infamy. In short, I had just learned what advantages are bestowed by education and idealism. It is not only the union of the sexes and the physical excitement of the nerves which bring this shiver of heavenly bliss, it is the spiritual emotion, the tension of all of the strength of the soul and abandon of all reason which procure this magical beautitude by lifting every fiber above its earthly activity. If I had seen this couple before the rich spectacle which my father and mother had offered me, my inclinations and my experiences would subsequently have been quite different. I understood clearly that we are not merely the playthings of chance, but that our virtues and vices are formed by the impressions which we receive. But for Marguerite I should probably soon have married, and but for my chance experience in the alcove I should have remained a virgin until then. This conviction, that we are dependent upon outside impressions and that we cannot voluntarily avoid them, permitted me to be kind and indulgent towards other people. What seems wrong at first glance is often no longer wrong if one takes the trouble to find out the reasons and the circumstances behind it.

The first part of the time that I spent in Vienna was noticeably unhappy. We knew scarcely anyone and I assiduously followed the singing lessons of my excellent professor. My one distraction consisted of trips to the theatre when operas were given.

However, I had many opportunities to make friends. I was in the full flower of youth and was courted by many young men, but my new-found reason had worked everything out. Before all else, I wanted to become a famous singer and only after that would I seek to enjoy myself. Nothing was to be allowed to upset the course of my studies, and I drove off my admirers with such severity that soon I was left completely alone. My elderly aunt was delighted by my virtuous conduct. It is true that she did not have the faintest suspicion of the secret amusements in which I moderately indulged.

I am coming now to a part of my confession which is much more difficult for me to relate than anything up to now, but I promised you that I would be sincere and so I am going to admit everything. I forgot to tell you that Marguerite had made me a present of the famous book, *Felicia, or My Adventures*, illustrated with aquatints, which by themselves would have taught me all about the center of all human activity if I had not already been initiated. This reading matter gave me the greatest pleasure. I allowed myself to read it only once a week, on Sunday evenings, when I took my hot bath, and when no one dared to disturb me. The bathroom was at the far end of the apartment and had only one door, which I covered in addition with a blanket in order to safeguard myself from any possible surprise. I was completely secure.

As I read the book in my bath, it had the same effect upon me as it had had on Marguerite. Who could possibly read these ardent descriptions without slipping into a fiery rapture? Once dried and lying down in my bathrobe, my own paradise, restricted though it was, opened its gates to me. I could see myself in full in the big mirror and my silent pleasure began with the admiration of every part of my body. I stroked and pressed my round young breasts, I played with their nipples, then my finger was led to the source of all feminine beautitudes.

My physical sensuality had matured rapidly and I had a very abundant flow of that balm, so sweet and intoxicating, which escapes from the depths of the feminine font at the moment of ecstasy. The men to whom I later gave myself were delighted with this precious quality. They could not sufficiently declare their utter pleasure when my jet inundated them. I believed then that this was common to all women, but in fact it is a rare gift. In Paris one of my most ardent admirers almost lost consciousness in his rapture when he felt my spring flood over him for the first time. Whenever I accorded him my favors after that, he withdrew hurriedly at the moment of ecstasy to bring his mouth to the eternal wound and drink deeply of the impetuous fountain, then came back with all the more ardor and discharged in his turn, but inside that little bladder such as Marguerite's Russian had used. This fantasy of my friend in Paris incited me in my turn to quaff of his jet which springs so wonderfully and so electrifyingly from the tree of life.

But this belongs to a later part of my confessions; let me come back to my evenings in Vienna.

I took immense pleasure in following in the mirror the lewd games of my hand. The center of sexual excitement was open to every attack because I parted my thighs as much as possible. I played busily, I rubbed and fondled, then I drove my finger in where it was so feverishly awaited.

Can one possibly recount the divine amusements that were derived from such activity? The blood whips through the veins, every nerve is roused, breath itself nearly ceases, and finally the dew of life gushes forth, rich and burning, to moisten and refresh the lips of the mouth of love. The memory of these ardent hours spent before a mirror in complete solitude in Vienna still delights me to such an extent that, as I write, my hand strays irresistibly to where this memory makes the most vivid impression. You will see by my wavering handwriting how much these feelings move me. My whole body trembles with pleasure and nostalgia. I throw down my pen! And . . .

VI

The description at the end of my last letter became too realistic and prevented me from continuing what I was going to say. The memory of the secret pleasures in which I indulged at the time of my virginal flowering wrenched the pen from my hand, and the latter once again played a role for me which even today has not lost its charms and to which I often turn even now as a result of my justifiable mistrust of men. I have probably already told you the worst, but I must still make a great effort to be honest in what is to follow. I have admitted that I regret nothing that I did to satisfy my sexual appetite, with the exception of my complete abandon of myself to that ruthless man who, but for your help, would have made me eternally unhappy, and so I am not sorry for what I did in Vienna towards the end of my studies in that city.

When I had made enough progress to be able to study operatic roles I needed an accompanist at the piano while I walked about the room practising my singing and my acting. My professor recommended a young musician who had just left a seminary. He was particularly interested in religious music and earned his living by giving lessons. A young man of about twenty, he was extremely shy, not very good-looking but possessed of a good figure, very clean, and dressed carefully like most of those who are educated in a religious institution. He was the only young man who was a regular visitor to the house, coming daily at lesson time, so it was perfectly natural that a familiarity of sorts should grow up between us.

He always kept his distance at first, was very shy and hardly ever dared even look at me. You know how mischievous and enterprising I am. I entertained myself by making him fall in love, a thing which I didn't find too difficult, since there is no better accomplice than music. It provides a thousand opportunities and as my talent appeared to the greatest advantage during these excercises I observed that gradually his feelings for me began to deepen.

I was not in love with him, for I only came to know that powerful sentiment much later, but I was amused to see how strong an influence I exercised upon a man still morally and physically pure. It was very cruel of me to indulge myself in this game, and as I realize that now, it becomes more difficult for me to tell you what happened.

After everything that I had seen, learned and

experienced, I was very keen to know more. My independent little mind wondered how to push Franz (that was his name) into something more decisive than sighs and languorous glances during my voice exercises, and when a woman is looking for a means to an end, she soon finds it. My old aunt used to go to market twice a week, usually leaving about the time my lessons were supposed to take place. When Franz arrived, the maid used to open the door to him without coming to announce him, because, she knew he was always expected. It was upon these facts that I had based my plan. Among other things, I told Franz that often I could not sleep at night and that if I lay down after lunch it was very difficult to wake me, for I slept so heavily.

Once that was established, I waited for him one day lying upon the sofa in a chosen pose. I lay back with one leg up, the back of it visible up to the garter. My *fichu*, of course, was disarranged and my throat and neck were bare. I had one arm folded across my eyes so that from underneath I could watch everything that Franz would do, and with thumping heart I awaited him, inwardly delighted to have arranged my clothes so well. I heard the kitchen door close and soon he walked in. He stopped in the doorway as if turned to stone, his face reddened and his eyes lit up. It seemed as if they should devour me at the sensitive place. The effect I had on him was so unquestionably apparent, even through his trousers, that for a moment I was afraid of being alone with him and entirely at his mercy. He coughed lightly, then louder to wake me up. As I made no sign he came closer to the sofa and cautiously bent down low enough to look under my skirts. I had arranged everything so that he shouldn't be wasting his time, but Franz told me later that he had only been able to see my thighs and nothing else. I watched all his actions, wanting to "sleep" as long as possible. He coughed again, then blew his nose very hard, and finally scraped some chairs about. I went on sleeping. He bent down over my bosom; next he peeped under my skirts. I remained asleep.

Suddenly he marched out of the room, either to leave or to look for the maid, poor dear. I, meanwhile, was growing annoyed at having prepared this scene in vain. (He declared to me later that he really had looked for the maid, but that she had evidently gone out.) A few minutes later he returned and seemed even more determined to wake me. He made a lot of noise, without any result of course, for I had made up my mind to win my case. He was very excited and seemed not to know what to do, but I had learned Marguerite's lessons and those of "Felicia" so well that I knew no man could resist such an opportunity for very long. Even if he had not had much experience, Franz still had senses, and he would have had to be made of stone to resist such a temptation. Finally, he actually plucked up courage enough to touch the calves of my legs, then my knees, then my thighs which were bare. If this contact excited me so much already, what sort of state must he have been in? Poor young man, with his eyes fixed fearfully upon my face in case I should wake up, he at last dared to touch the place which attracted him so powerfully.

A thrill ran over me when, for the first time, I felt a male hand at the center of all my pleasures. This was something different from anything I had ever known, and I was no longer play-acting when I began to sigh. I shifted myself slightly but not to the disadvantage of my poor trembling knight. He thought for a moment that I was going to wake up, then, convinced that I really was sound asleep, began his play again. Thanks to my new position he had a much greater opportunity, so that he was no longer content just to touch me lightly. Gently he lifted up my skirts in order to see better. You told me yourself, when you were examining me, that in spite of the ravages of that disgusting disease I was very well shaped in that place, so you can well imagine that Franz was beside himself when his hands revealed everything. As gently as possible, he stroked the object of his and, I must admit, my own desires. It was then that I realized the great difference between the hand of a man and that of Marguerite or myself. Fast "asleep" as I was, I stretched myself out, turning and twisting, but all the time careful not to close my legs, although that would have been the most natural thing for a sleeping woman to do.

Franz could no longer control himself. He hastily opened his trousers and bared his weapon, which surely would have conquered me if I had not suddenly remembered Marguerite's warnings. I wanted to become a great actress. That was my unshakeable resolution, but I was equally determined to enjoy all that a woman might taste without danger. There could be no question, then, of giving myself up to an inexperienced youth, so I "woke up" just as he was kneeling down between my thighs. With horror-filled eyes, I stared at the foolhardy one and, in one sideways movement, stole from him all the advantages of his position.

You have always praised my great talent as an actress. Here, then, was a splendid scene in which you would have admired the way I can play a role. On one side, reproaches, disappointment, tears; on the other, fright, embarrassment and shame. He even forgot to hide the real traitor of the situation, an oversight I found very agreeable, for in the midst of my tears and sobs I was able to satisfy my curiosity. I had every reason to congratulate myself on my little comedy, for I had just won a very robust young man. The explanation was a very simple one. I made him see that he had dishonored me and that he would have to leave town if I were to complain of his disgraceful behavior. I told him that I would have chased him away and that he could never have come back except for the fact that I had a weakness for him and that for a long time I had been aware of his love. I forgave him his error because of his great passion, and I told him all this with such conviction and in so straightforward a manner that he believed every word. He calmed down, little by little, finally hiding that which denounced too visibly his crime, and all ended in a passionate, lingering kiss.

Things went no further that day; he was as timid as before and dared make no other move. After all the reproaches, the declarations, the pardons, he continued as if nothing had happened. Our singing lesson was incredibly dull and when my aunt came back from market, Franz left me, happy and fearful. However, I realized that he would never come back, but I did not want to admit such a grave error. I was worried and distraught, and I wracked my brain to find a means for getting my way without risking my honor. Above all, I had to be alone with him again. I had guessed rightly, as he admitted later, for he had decided never to return again. It was not difficult for me to do everything I wished, for I did not love him—I was simply determined to have my own way.

My singing professor served unwittingly as a go-between. I asked him to examine me to see if I had made progress with the accompanist he had recommended. Franz of course had to be present at this examination and was amazed to find himself suddenly face to face with me once again. I told him surreptitiously that I had to see him, and that my aunt or the maid must have noticed something. He was very worried and ready to do anything, and I arranged to meet him that evening at the theatre. Now when young people begin to have secret rendezvouses, the rest follows quite naturally. A great stride had been made. That evening I left my box as usual and met Franz in the appointed place. I told him that according to the strange allusions which my aunt had made, the maid must have been spying on us, and that I was desperate because I didn't know what he had been doing while I was asleep nor to what lengths his audacity had carried him. I told him further that since then I had not been feeling well, that I had been feverish, and that I suspected the worst. Franz didn't know how to reassure me. By this time we had come very close to the house where I lived, and suddenly, when my distraction had reached its limits, I pretended to half faint and no longer be capable of walking another step. Franz was obliged to look for a cab, and if I hadn't made him get into it he would actually have let me continue home by myself. In the dark narrow confines of the cab, however, he could no longer elude me. The minutes fled rapidly by, and I told him that I could not face my aunt like this, in tears and all untidy, and I asked him to tell the driver to take us to the river bank.

From then on things went better. Tears changed into kisses, reproaches into caresses. For the first time I felt the charm of a man's arms around me. I defended myself, but weakly, for his timidity would have made him stop at once. I still wanted to know what he had been doing while I was asleep. When he saw that his explanations and affirmations did not convince me, he tried to prove that he had been content with little. His hand sought the place which had been waiting for him so long. His first touch brought me quite a different sensation than when I had been "asleep," for this time he was kissing my mouth also. I squeezed my thighs together as tightly as possible, and only relaxed them little by little as if I were yielding to his caresses. I sighed, my reproaches ceased as my breath grew shorter, and I enjoyed the tenderness of his hands, even though they were very clumsy and inexperienced. As for me, I knew better how to reach the right place and provoke the moment of delight. Franz did not know that in a woman the sensibility is greatest at the entry of the sanctuary. He was still trying to thrust his finger in as deeply as possible, and the more he succeeded, the more excited he became. I was well aware that nature was driving him to complete what he had begun and to give himself to me completely, but there could be no question of that, and certainly never between us. So when he pressed me too closely and tried to explore further I repulsed him in a lively fashion and threatened to call for help. I was tolerant and good-natured again when he moved away in fright and contented himself with what I could give him. I was highly pleased with the success of my plan, even though this pleasure was still incomplete. I had taken the cab to help me get over my indisposition, but our activities hardly permitted it. In the end I had to hurry to get home on time.

I left Franz feeling sure that I would see him again soon and I was not wrong. He did come and then began a succession of happy pleasure-filled hours. Even today, they are among my most beautiful memories, though I have since known other delights more intense and more rich.

Once while I was staying with the family of the proprietor of a large estate who possessed a stud farm of English and Arab horses, I was present nearly every day at the revels of these admirable stallions when they covered the mares. The first time it was by accident that I was there, but the vision I witnessed remained unforgettable. Thanks to my natural slyness I was able to enjoy this spectacle over a period of three weeks while my friends were away to take the waters. No one suspected that hidden behind a curtain I watched the stallions, for my room did not look out upon the enclosures. I do not know if you have ever seen this act taking place between thoroughbred horses, but I can assure you that there is nothing more beautiful than a stallion covering a mare. Their wonderful form, their strength, the fire in their eyes, the visible tension of all the nerves, of all the muscles, and finally their frenzy amounting to rage, all of this has for me a magical attraction. One may remain unmoved, even be disgusted, or speak of such things with disdain, but one is forced to admit that copulation is the supreme moment of animal life. Birds sing with more fervor, stags fight, every creature grows in strength and beauty, and all of this is to be seen personified particularly in thoroughbred horses. The mare, obeying a law of nature, refuses herself, and the stallion must approach her very carefully in order to avoid the danger of being kicked or nipped. Little by little, he manages to overcome her resistance. He gallops around her, rubs her flanks with his nose, whinnies and does not know how to use up his surplus strength. Under his velvety coat all the veins and all the muscles swell, and the sign of virility appears in all its grandeur. You cannot see where it is going to be thrust in. In the end the mare accepts and presents herself. In the twinkling of an eye, the stallion attacks furiously. For a long time he struggles in vain, for the target is too small for the blows of such a lance. You feel that you would like to help the poor beast and that the stable-boys do. But he has hardly touched the edge of it, the mare has hardly taken in the tip of it, when there follows such a thrust as to defy description. His eyes start out of their sockets, steam rises in clouds out of his nostrils, and his entire body seems to be convulsed. Anybody who is watching at this point will experience a penetrating thrill, and I cannot deny that I used to feast my eyes upon this spectacle and that it always stimulated me immensely. Let me come back to my subject at once.

After the declarations and the intimacies in the cab, my affair with Franz took on a very special aspect. As I did not love him, for I only came to know that powerful feeling much later, to my great misfortune, I was determined never to allow him all the rights of a husband. He was only to be an amusement for me. With him I wanted to learn and experiment in everything which I might safely try. Of course, he gradually became more daring, but as I never permitted him everything I was always able to dominate and rule him.

Whenever I was alone with him I spent the most exquisite hours. I let him take the greatest liberties and soon he was no longer as inexpert and as timid as in the cab. He finally dared to kiss every part of my body—to kiss them and delight in them. It is true that he made it very difficult for me to prevent him going further, however. When he tried to wriggle in between my thighs, suddenly get his trousers off and reach the principal goal, I had to push him away, and I was only nice to him again when he promised to be less demanding.

The poor thing found this very trying. I noticed several times that he could not control his excitement and that he discharged his strength very quickly. For a long time I had been very curious to see at closer quarters that admirable member. Of course, it would not have done for him to notice what I wanted so much. On the contrary, he had to believe that it was he who was leading me step by step down this slippery path. The best way to let him do everything that I wanted him to. My aunt's little dog had taught me that if you cannot have everything you want, certain compensations are always possible. So I had no trouble in inducing Franz to kiss not only my mouth and breasts, but to choose a more sensitive object for his kisses. When my sighs, palpitations and tremors showed him that I had a weakness for that sort of caress, he became even more devoted and brought me even more delights. Sometimes he seemed to want to take advantage of me when, after the flooding of my inside, I was prostrated and overcome by a complete abandon. He would then climb between my thighs, hoping to profit by a moment of inattention. He was disappointed every time, because even during the greatest ecstasy I never lost sight of everything I would be risking by yielding to him.

I now knew and tasted everything that Marguerite had enjoyed with her mistress. When Franz was lying between my legs and his tongue played the wildest and most lascivious games, tickled me, sucked me and tried to thrust itself in as far as possible, and when, lying there tranquilly, I took an untroubled pleasure, I compared myself to the baroness and thought myself much more happy than she, for I had a strong, handsome young man, while she had only had Marguerite. Franz was admirable, especially at the moment of the strongest thrill, when the warm flood sprang from my interior and he did not draw his lips away, but on the contrary pressed them even closer and drank as though he would have absorbed all my life. This kind of pleasure had always had an extraordinary attraction for me, and is probably connected with the complete passivity of the woman, who receives a man's caresses and with it the homage rendered to her charm. Even in a simple kiss, the effect is more than intoxicating, but if the tongue also knows its duty or has learned it through the quivering of the parts that are caressed, I honestly do not know whether I do not prefer this pleasure to all others. Then again, it lasts longer and is not satiating.

What is to follow is even more difficult for me to admit, but we have agreed that I would be truthful to the smallest detail, and what I could never tell you orally must be written down. It was quite natural that after each amiability and compliance on Franz' part there should be reciprocity on mine. For a long time I had wanted to do what I had seen my mother accomplish on that unforgettable day when she had stimulated my father to repeat their pleasures before my very eyes. It was something easily realized. First the hand, turning the eyes away as if ashamed, then the mouth, still hesitating, then becoming more and more appreciative, and at last the whole pleasure quite shamelessly. I do not know what feelings men have when they caress all the objects of their desires, but if I dare to draw conclusions from what I felt in looking at, caressing, and kissing this marvelous symbol of manly strength, then in sucking it and provoking the sudden jet of life-giving fluid, really the man's pleasure must be enormous.

What I now saw and touched I had already seen in my father, my cousin and my parent's coachman, but I was to know it in all the proportions of its strength and beauty. Franz was younger than my father, healthier and stronger than my cousin, much more pleasant and tender than the rough stableman. Probably there are many women who through modesty or prudishness, never appreciate the whole of the pleasure. That depends upon many things: first of all upon the woman's nature, then upon the violence of the man, who, sometimes only lingers involuntarily upon the preludes—even though they are so pleasant—and who strives immediately towards the final rapture. As far as Franz was concerned this compensation, since I constantly barred him from what he called his paradise, was well-deserved and overdue. In any case, he was so excited by the time he had kissed me, sucked and drank of my fountain of love, that out of mere pity I would have had to do what I was now doing for pleasure.

My own pleasures were formerly curtailed when he became so excited that only two or three movements of my hand often sufficed to relieve him of the overflow of his strength. On the other hand, I felt a great deal of pleasure when, after a short pause and careful washing, he was reborn little by little in my mouth, when this masterpiece of nature recovered its strength. How it grew and how red it was! How tender he was and how helpless after the fulfillment; how delightful it was at the moment of the jet! Must I, after having said so much, hide the fact that in a moment of intoxication I covered the tender tip of it, that I received all of the fluid in my mouth, and that I did not stop sucking and drinking until the last drop of this divine balm had flowed! Even today the blood surges in my veins when I think about it, and I really do not regret anything that I did then. What I did later gave me cause for bitter remorse, and I owe it to your unselfish friendship that this remorse has not poisoned the rest of my life. As I found out for myself, one cannot play with fire with impunity, and the strongest principles may be overthrown by a momentary shudder of the nerves, an evil genius inside of us. It would be very sad if any young girl reading these letters were to wish to act as I did in these rather unusual circumstances. If, for example, she gave herself up several times a week to solitary pleasures, however voluptuous they might be, physical weaknesses and sickness would follow. If she entrusted herself to the intimate companionship of a woman-friend without first assuring herself of this woman's discretion she would run into all sorts of difficulties. If she allowed a young man who did not intend to marry her all manner of favors, and that without being in full control of her senses, she would make herself unhappy for the rest of her life.

Marriage is a reasonable institution which every reasonable man must defend. Without marriage, sensual desires would make savage beasts of men. This is my conviction, even though I am not myself married. An actress dare not have any ties. She cannot be at the same time a housewife, a mother and the idol of the public. I feel that I would naturally be a conscientious wife and a very tender mother if my husband made me happy, as I deserve, and it is because I know the extraordinary importance of sexual life in all human conditions, because I know by experience and observation that this point, kept secret by the most honorable and tender men, is the center of the life of a society, and it is because of all this that I would be an exemplary helpmate. I would act as my mother had acted, I would make an effort to be always new for my husband. I would lend myself to all his fantasies, and yet I would still always keep something from him; I would be without ever seeming to be, which is, I believe, the key to all human happiness.

VII

You must have found me very serious as you read the end of my last letter, but that is just another trait of my character. I always seem to be able to foresee the way a chain of events will unroll, and take into account the various impressions, feelings and experiences that go to make it up. Even the most violent intoxication of the senses has never been able to make me lose my critical facilities, and today, in fact, I am beginning a chapter of my confessions which will prove this statement.

My affair with Franz continued. I was always very prudent and so my aunt suspected nothing and our rendezvouses were secret from all those around us. In addition, I refused to be alone with Franz more than once a week. The day of my debut was drawing near and Franz was becoming more and more rash. He thought he had obtained some rights over me, and he was becoming too domineering, like all men who believe themselves sure of an undisputed possession, but this was not how I intended it to be, and I immediately conceived a plan. At the beginning of a brilliant career was I to connect myself with a man of no importance, one to whom I was, on all points, superior? To leave him on bad terms, however, would have been dangerous, for I would then be at the mercy of his indiscretion. It was necessary to be very clever, which I was, for I succeeded in ending our liaison so opportunely and so deceptively that Franz still believes today that if chance had not separated us I would certainly have married him.

The "chance" was my doing. I had informed my professor that my accompanist had pursued me with his declarations and that I was ready to break off the course of my artistic career in exchange for love in a cottage. However, the good man, who was extremely proud of his pupil and who was counting heavily on my debut, grew very angry. I begged him not to make Franz miserable, and so I reached my goal while Franz reached the Budapest Theatre Orchestra by special engagement. We bade each other a tender farewell; I had broken off my relations without anything to fear.

Shortly after our separation I gave my first performance at the Theatre of the Kärntnertor, and you know how successful it was. I was more than happy. I was surrounded and besieged. Applause, money and celebrity poured my way and I had plenty of suitors, admirers and enthusiasts. Some thought to reach their aim with poems and some with valuable presents, but I had already observed that an artist cannot give in to his vanity or his feeling without risking everything in the game. This is why I pretended to be indifferent. I discouraged all those who came near me and soon acquired the reputation of a woman of unassailable virtue. Nobody had any idea that after Franz's departure I turned again to my solitary joys on Sunday evenings and to the delights of the hot bath. However, I never yielded more than once a week to the call of my senses, although they demanded much more. A thousand eyes were upon me and so I was extremely prudent in my relationships. My aunt had to go everywhere with me and nobody could accuse me of a single indiscretion.

This lasted all winter long. I had a steady income, and I installed myself in a very comfortable and well-furnished apartment. I was accepted in the best society and found myself very happy with my new life. I only regretted rarely Franz's departure, and fortunate circumstances compensated me for it the following summer.

I had been introduced into the house of one of the richest bankers in Vienna, and I received from his wife all of the marks of the truest friendship. Her husband had paid court to me, hoping with his huge fortune to easily conquer a popular actress. When he had been driven away like all the others, he introduced me to his household, thinking to win me that way. Thus it came about that I could come and go there as I pleased. I consistently repulsed his advances and, perhaps, because of that, his wife soon became my most intimate friend. Roudolphine, for that was her name, was about twenty-seven years old, a piquant brunette, very vivacious, lively, tender and very much a woman. She had no children and was quite indifferent to her husband, of whose misdemeanors she was painfully aware. The relationship between them was friendly, and they did not refuse themselves from time to time the joys of marriage. Yet, in spite of all, it was not a happy union. Her husband probably did not realize that she was a very warm-blooded woman, a fact she most likely concealed very skillfully.

At the approach of the fine weather, Roudolphine went to live in a charming villa at Baden where her husband used to visit her regularly every Sunday, bringing a few friends with him. She invited me to spend the summer there with her at the end of the theatre season. This stay in the country was to do me a lot of good. Until then we had only talked about clothes, music and art, but now our conversations began to assume a different character. The court that her husband paid me provided her the opportunity for this. I noticed that she measured her husband's misbehavior according to the privations which he imposed upon her. Her complaints were so sincere, and she hid so little the object of her regret, that I immediately concluded that I had been chosen as her confidant and decided to act like a simple and inexperienced friend. I had played my cards right and touched upon her weakness; she at once began to explain things to me, and the more innocent I pretended to be and the more I seemed astounded by what she told me, the more she insisted on fully informing me of what filled her heart.

In addition, she took great pleasure in revealing certain physical matters to me. She was utterly astounded at the surprise I showed at discovering these things. She could not believe that a young artist who was always playing with fire could be so unaware of everything. It was only the fourth day after my arrival when we took a bath together—practical instruction could hardly be left out after so many fine speeches—and the more I appeared clumsy and self-conscious, the more amusement she derived from exercising a novice. The more difficulties I made, the more passionate she grew. However, in the bath and during the day she did not dare go beyond certain familiarities, and I realized that she was going to employ all of her cunning to persuade me to spend the night with her. The memory of the first night spent in Marguerite's bed obsessed me in such a way that I was quite ready to yield to her wish. I did this with such a show of ingenuousness that she was more and more convinced of my innocence. She thought she was seducing me, but it was I who was getting my way.

She had the most charming bedroom, furnished with all the luxuries that only a wealthy banker can afford, and with all the taste of a room arranged for a wedding night. It was there that Roudolphine had become a woman. She recounted in detail her experience and what had been her feelings when the flower of her innocence had been taken. She made no secret of the fact that she was very sensual. She also told me that until her second confinement she had never found any pleasure in her husband's embraces, which were then very frequent. Her pleasures, which developed only gradually, had suddenly become very intense. For a long time I could not believe that, having been very ardent myself ever since my youth, but I believe it now. In most cases this situation is the husband's fault; he is in too much of a hurry to finish as soon as he enters, and does not know how to excite his wife's sensuality first, or else he gives up half way.

Roudolphine had compensations; she was charming and avid and only bore her husband's negligence with all the more bad humor. I shall not bother to tell you all the sports in which we engaged in her big English bed. Our revels were delightful, lascivious, and Roudolphine was insatiable in the pleasure she took in kisses and the contact of our two naked bodies. She enjoyed herself for two hours and hardly suspected that these hours were still too short for me, so much did I desire and so much did I pretend to yield only with difficulty and shame.

Our relationship soon became much more interesting, for Roudolphine consoled herself in secret for her husband's pranks. In the neighboring town lived an Italian prince who usually stayed in Vienna where Roudolphine's husband looked after his financial affairs. The banker was the humble servant of the prince's huge fortune. The latter, about thirty years old, was outwardly a very severe and a very proud man with a scientific education and turn of mind; inwardly, however, he was dominated by the most intense sensuality. Nature had gifted him with exceptional physical strength. In addition, he was the most complete egotist I have ever met. He had but one aim in life, pleasure at all costs, and but one law, to preserve himself by dint of subterfuge from all the troublesome consequences of his affairs. When the banker was there, the prince often came to dine or to tea.

I had never noticed, however, that there was any affair between him and Roudolphine. I learned about it entirely by chance, for she was very careful never to breathe a word of it to me. The gardens of their two villas were adjacent, and one day when I was picking flowers behind a hedge I saw Roudolphine pluck a note from underneath a stone, conceal it quickly in her blouse and hurry away to her room. Suspecting some little intrigue, I peeped through her window and saw her hastily read and burn it. Then she sat down at her desk, I supposed, to compose the answer. So that she would suspect nothing, I hastened to my room and began to sing at the top of my voice, at the same time carefully watching the place in the garden where the note had been left. Soon Roudolphine appeared, walked along the hedge toying with the branches, then so swiftly and adroitly did she hide her reply that I did not catch her at it. However, I had noticed the spot where she had paused the longest, and as soon as she had returned to the house, and when I was certain that she was busy, I dashed into the garden. I easily found the message hidden under a stone. Back in my room with the door locked I read, "Not today, Pauline is sleeping with me. I will tell her tomorrow that I am indisposed. For you, of course, I am not. Come tomorrow, then, as usual, at eleven o'clock."

The note was in Italian and in disguised handwriting. You can well imagine that everything was at once clear to me. I had already made up my mind what to do. I did not return the note to where I had found it, for I wanted the prince to come that night and surprise us both in bed. I, the *ingènue*, was in possession of Roudolphine's secret and I felt sure I would not come out of the situation empty handed. Of course, I still did not know how the prince would manage to get to Roudolphine's bedroom.

At lunch we had agreed to spend the night together, which is why she had refused the prince's visit. Over tea she explained to me that we could not sleep together for about a week, for she felt that her period was approaching. She thought this would delude me, but I had already woven my net around her. Above all, I had to get her to bed before eleven o'clock, so that she could find no means of avoiding, at the last minute, the surprise I had prepared for her.

We went to bed very early, and I was so frolicsome, so caressing, and so insatiable that she soon went to sleep out of sheer fatigue. Bosom against bosom, her thighs between mine, our hands reciprocally at the sources of our pleasure we lay there, she fast asleep and I more and more wide awake and impatient. I had blown out the lamp and waited excitedly. Suddenly I heard the floor of the alcove creak, the sound of muffled footsteps, and the door opened. I heard someone breathing, getting undressed, and at last approaching the bed on Roudolphine's side.

Now I was sure of myself, and I pretended to be very deeply asleep. The prince, for it was he, lifted up the bedclothes and lay down beside Roudolphine, who woke up terrified. I felt her trembling all over. Now came the catastrophe. He wanted to ascend immediately to the throne he had so many times possessed. She stopped him, asking hastily whether or not he had received her reply. Meanwhile, trying to get where he wanted, he had touched my hand and my arm. I cried out, I was beside myself, shuddering and pressing myself against Roudolphine. I was highly diverted by her fright and the prince's amazement. He had shouted an Italian oath, so that it was no use for Roudolphine to explain that it was her husband coming unexpectedly to surprise her. I overwhelmed her with reproaches and upbraided her with having exposed my youth and honor to such a dreadful scene, because I had recognized the princes' voice. The prince, a gallant and knowing man, soon realized, however, that he had nothing to lose. On the contrary, he was gaining an interesting partner. That was just what I expected him to think. After a few tender and amusing words he went to close the bedroom door, took out the keys, and returned to bed.

Roudolphine was between us. Now came the excuses, the explanations and the recriminations. But there was nothing to be done, nothing could be changed; we would have to keep quiet, all three of us, in order not to expose ourselves to the unpleasant consequences of so hazardous a meeting, a thing it would be hard to explain. Roudolphine calmed down little by little and the prince's words grew sweeter and sweeter. I, of course, was in floods of tears. By my reproaches I forced Roudolphine to make me her confidant and thus her accomplice in this illegal liaison. You can see that Marguerite's lessons and her adventures in Geneva were useful to me. In fact, it was exactly the same story except that the prince and Roudolphine did not realize that they were merely puppets in my hands.

Roudolphine, then, no longer tried to hide from me the facts of her long-standing liaison with the prince, but she also revealed to him what she had been doing with me, the innocent young girl, and she told him how I burned with desire to learn more of these matters. That excited the prince and when I tried to make Roudolphine be quiet she only talked with all the more ardor of my sensuality! I noticed that he was pressing his thighs between those of Roudolphine and was trying in this way to reach the desired goal from the side. From time to time his legs brushed against mine, and I wept, I burned with curiosity. Roudolphine tried to console me, but with every movement the prince made she became more and more distraught. Soon she too squirmed about, trembled passionately, and finally moved her hand to my body to try to make me share her pleasure. Suddenly I noticed another hand straying where hers was already so busy. I could not allow that to continue, for I wanted to remain faithful to the role which I had given myself, so I turned over angrily towards the wall and, as Roudolphine had immediately taken away her own hand when she encountered that of her lover on this forbidden path, I was abandoned to my sulking and I myself had to finish secretly what my bed companion had begun.

Hardly had I turned my back on them when they forgot all restraint and all shame. The prince threw himself upon Roudolphine, who opened her legs as wide as possible to receive the beloved guest easily and quickly, and the bed shook at every movement. I was so consumed with desire and envy; I could not see anything, but my imagination was aflame. Then at the moment when the two lovers were fused most closely and overflowed, sighing and shuddering, I myself let loose so abundant a burning flood that I lost consciousness.

After the practical exercise came the theory. The prince was now between Roudolphine and myself, although I do not know whether this was by design or accident. He did not make the slightest movement, and I seemed to have nothing to fear, but I was perfectly aware that I had to keep quiet in order to maintain my superiority, and I waited to see what they would do next. Roudolphine explained to me first that, since her husband neglected her and ran after other women, she had every right to give herself freely to a cavalier so pleasant, so courtly, and above all, so discreet. She was in the best years of her life and did not want, indeed she was not able, to miss all the sweetest of earthly joys, especially since her doctors had advised her not to attempt to repress her natural sensuality. In any case, I knew that she was a very warm-natured woman, and she was sure that I was not indifferent to love, but only afraid of the consequences. She said that she simply wanted to remind me of what we had been doing together that evening before the unexpected arrival of the prince. I wanted to put my hand over her mouth to shut her up, but I could not do this without making a motion towards my neighbor, who seized my hand immediately and covered it with tender little kisses.

Now it was his turn to talk. His was not an easy role as he had to weigh every word so as not to hurt Roudolphine's feelings, but I realized by the intonation of his voice that he was more anxious to win me as quickly as possible than he was concerned about upsetting Roudolphine. However, by this time she was obliged to put up with anything in order to keep her secret.

I no longer remember what the prince said to soothe me, to excuse himself, and to prove that I had nothing to fear. I only remember that the warmth of his body was driving me crazy, that his hand was stroking first my breasts, then the rest of my body, and finally the very center of his desires and mine. The state I was in defies description. The prince advanced slowly but surely; however, I could not allow him to kiss me, for he would then have noticed how I burned with desire to return his caresses. I was struggling with myself; I wanted to have done with this comedy, to put an end to my affected modesty, and to surrender entirely to the situation, but if I did that I would lose my advantage over the two sinners, and I would have been exposed to the dangers of love making with this violent and passionate man; for the prince would not have known how to limit his triumph once he was the victor.

I had noticed how feverishly he had finished with Roudolphine. All my entreaties would have been in vain, and perhaps even a backward movement would not have helped me. Besides, how could I tell whether, at the last moment, I would have been able to restrain myself? My whole artistic career was at stake, but I held my ground and let him do almost anything to me without responding to it, only defending myself desperately when the prince tried to obtain more. Roudolphine was at a loss as to what to say to me, or what she should do herself. She realized that my resistance had to be broken that night if she were going to be able to look me in the eyes the following day. To excite me even more, which was really quite unnecessary, she lay her head upon my bosom, embraced me, licked my breasts, and finally hurled herself between my legs where she pressed her lips to the still-inviolate entry of the temple, and began a play so pleasant that I allowed her complete freedom. The prince had yielded his place to her, and he was now kissing me on the mouth.

Thus I was covered from head to foot with kisses. I was no longer making any attempt to resist, so he placed my hand upon his scepter, and I permitted this familiarity unenthusiastically. My arm passed between the thighs of Roudolphine, who was kneeling, and I noticed that the prince's other hand was now in the place where his scepter had been reveling so short a time before. He taught me to caress it, to rub and squeeze it. The group we formed was complicated but extremely pleasant; it was dark and I was sorry not to be able to see, for one must enjoy these things with the eyes as well. Roudolphine was trembling, excited to the extreme by the kisses she was showering upon me and the caresses she was receiving from the prince. She was half senseless with delight and opened wide her legs, whereupon the prince suddenly straightened himself and took up a position which was thus far unknown to me, bending over and penetrating her from behind. I had pulled my hand away, but he seized it and brought it to the point where he was most intimately united with Roudolphine. He then taught me an occupation which I should never have dreamed of, and which enhanced the rapture of the two pleasure-seekers. I was now to squeeze the root of his dagger and now to caress the sheath which enclosed it. Although I pretended to be ashamed, I was in fact extremely zealous in doing this. Roudolphine kissed and licked passionately and, all three together, we soared quickly to the very summit of pleasure. It was so intoxicating that it took us a good quarter of an hour to recover ourselves. We felt much too hot, and on this summer night we could stand neither the contact of each other's bodies nor that of the bedclothes and we lay naked as far apart as we could.

After this passionate and sweltering action the discussion was resumed anew. The prince talked as calmly about this strange chance rendezvous as if he had organized a party in the country. Basing his assumptions on what Roudolphine had told him, he no longer took the trouble to win me, contenting himself simply with combating my fear of unhappy consequences. He was well aware that he would have no difficulty in convincing me. The virtuosity of my hand, the pleasure which I had tasted and which had been betrayed by my beating heart and the trembling of my thighs had revealed to him how sensual I was. He only had to prove to me that there was no danger and that is what he was trying to do with all the art of a man of the world.

For these reasons he imagined that it would only be a question of time. He therefore did not insist upon the repetition of such a night and soon left us, for dawn was in the offing. He was perfectly willing to sacrifice the length of time spent in pleasure in order to safeguard his secret and his safety. He had to go through the dressing room and a corridor, climb a ladder, go out through a window, crawl back in through a skylight before finding himself in his house again, from where he would have to creep steathily back to his apartments. The leave-taking was a strange mixture of intimacy, tenderness, timidity, teasing and deference, and when he had left, neither Roudolphine nor I felt like talking things over any more. We were so tired that we fell asleep at once. Later, upon awakening, I pretended to be inconsolable at having fallen into the hands of a man, but I was really furious that she had told him about our pleasures. She did not even notice how much delight I found in her efforts to console me.

Naturally, I refused to sleep with her the next night, telling her that my senses were never to lead me astray from my good resolutions another time, for I never wanted such a thing to happen again; I wanted to sleep by myself, and she was not to believe that I would ever permit the prince to do what she allowed him to do so easily. She was married and it would do no harm if she became pregnant, but I was an artist. A thousand eyes were upon me, and I did not dare do anything like that, which would bring me to disaster.

As I had expected, she then spoke to me about safety measures. She told me she had met the prince at a time when she was not sleeping with her husband because of a quarrel, and that consequently, she did not dare to become pregnant. The prince had calmed all her fears by using condoms, and she told me that I could try them too. She also told me she was quite sure that the prince was very level-headed and had perfect control of his feelings. In any case, he knew another way of preserving a lady's honor and, if I were very nice to him, I would soon learn about it. In short, she tried by every means to persuade me to surrender to the prince, so that I might enjoy the gayest and happiest of hours. I gave her to understand that her explanations and her promises did not leave me entirely cold, but that I was still rather fearful.

Towards noon the prince came to visit Roudolphine, a polite visit which also included me. But I feigned illness and did not appear. This gave them the chance to agree freely upon the measures to take to overcome my resistance and to initiate me into their secret games. As I did not want to sleep with Roudolphine any more, they would probably arrange to surprise me in my bedroom as quickly as possible, so as not to leave me time to repent, and perhaps to go back to town. My surprise proved correct.

All that afternoon and evening, Roudolphine did not mention previous nights to me. She came up to my bedroom that night, however, and sent away the chambermaid. When I was in bed, she went to lock up the anteroom herself so that nobody would disturb us. Then she sat down on my bed and tried to convince me anew. She described everything to me in the most beautiful and seductive manner and assured me there was nothing to fear. Of course, I pretended that I did not know the prince was in her room and that he might even be listening from behind the door, so I had to be prudent and give in to her arguments little by little.

"But who is to guarantee to me that the prince will use the mask which you described?"

"I will. Do you think that I would let him do anything more with you than what I let him do with me at first? I promise you that he will not appear without a mask at this ball."

"But it must hurt terribly. You know he guided my hand and made me feel his strength."

"At the very beginning it may really hurt you, but there are remedies for that, too. You have some oil of almonds and some cold cream. We will smear his lance with them so that he can penetrate more easily."

"Are you quite sure that no drop of that dangerous liquid can get through to bring about my misfortune?"

"Come now, do you think that I would have given in without that assurance? Everything was at stake then, as I had no contacts at all with my husband at that time. When I had made up with him I permitted the prince everything. But now I arrange things so that he visits me at least once every time the prince has been here. And so I have nothing to fear any longer."

"The thought of that misfortune horrifies me. Besides, there is still the shame of giving oneself to a man. I do not know what to do. Everything you say charms me, and my senses are urging me to take your advice, but for nothing in the world would I put up with another night like the last, for I know that I should never be able to resist again. You are quite right. The prince is as gallant as he is handsome, and you will never know what feelings were aroused in me when I heard the sounds of your surrender there beside me."

"I too had a double pleasure in letting you share, although very imperfectly, in what I was feeling myself. I should never have thought that pleasure among three could be as violent as that which I tasted myself last night. I had read about it in books, but I always thought that it was exaggerated. The thought of a woman sharing herself between two men is odious to me, but I think that the accord between two women and a sensible, discreet man is delightful; but of course the two women must be true friends. One of them must not be more timid and more fearful than the other, and that is still your trouble, Pauline, dear."

"It is just as well that your prince is not here, my dear, to hear your conversation. I really shouldn't know how to resist him, for I am totally consumed by what you have been telling me. Just look how I am burning, here, and how I am trembling all over."

As I spoke, I uncovered myself—part of my thighs—and placed myself in such a position that if anyone were looking through the keyhole he would not miss a thing. If the prince were really there this was the moment for him to come in—and he did.

As you might have expected of an experienced and perfect man of the world, he understood at once that no talking was necessary, that he should conquer first and talk about it later. By the way Roudolphine had behaved I could see that everything had been arranged in advance. I tried to hide under the bedclothes, but she pulled them off me; I started to weep and she laughingly smothered me with kisses. Although at last I expected the immediate fulfillment of the desire which had been mine for so long, I still had to be patient, for I had reckoned without Roudolphine's jealousy. In spite of the necessity of making me her accomplice, in spite of the fear of seeing her plans come to naught at the last minute, she was not going to sacrifice to me the first fruits of this day's pleasure. With an expression on her face that I envied, but which I dared not unmask if I were to stay within my own role, she told the prince that I had consented and that I was ready to do anything, but that I wanted to be certain of the efficiency of the means used, and that she would like to submit to a demonstration in front of me.

It was obvious that the prince was not expecting such an offer, and that he would have preferred to have carried out this trial directly with me rather than with Roudolphine. She took several of the small bladders from her pocket, breathed into one to show that it was impermeable, then moistened it and put it on with many caresses and giggles. After that she quickly undressed and lay down on the bed beside me, pulling the prince down on top of her, and exhorting me to watch closely so that I would lose all fear.

And so I really did see everything. I saw the delight of this handsome couple. I saw his strength and his power; I saw him penetrate her, I saw her rise to meet him, and I saw them forget everything around them as the ecstasy grew until finally the flow took place amid sighs and shudders of delight.

Roudolphine did not relax the hold of her thighs before she had recovered her senses. Then with a beaming face she removed the condom and showed me triumphantly that not a single drop had overflowed. She took all the trouble imaginable to make me understand that which Marguerite had already explained to me so well, but which I had never been able to procure for myself. For in that case Franz could have used it, too.

Roudolphine overflowed with joy. She had demonstrated to me her supremacy and had gathered the first fruits of the prince, who had certainly been expecting another dish that evening. I decided that later I would take my revenge. The prince, however, was very kind. Instead of making the most of his advantage, he treated us both very tenderly. He took nothing, contenting himself with what we were ready to give him, and spoke with passion of the pleasure which divine chance had brought him in the persons of so charming a pair of women. Describing our relationship in the most glowing colors, he filled in the time that he needed to gather up his strength once more. He was no longer very young, but he was still valiant as a lover, and at last the moment arrived. He entreated me to trust myself to him absolutely. Roudolphine very prettily made the victor's toilet, while I watched, peeping through my fingers. The cold cream was lavishly applied, and at last the longed-for instant arrived: I was going to receive a man. For a long time I had been wondering how I was going to deceive the prince about my virginity, because the first time I had used Marguerite's instrument I had lost that which men prize so highly.

As I wanted to surrender myself and since I had consented to be the third person in their games, I felt that I should behave myself without false modesty, and I let my two companions do all that they desired to me. Roudolphine laid me down on the bed in such a position that my head was leaning against the wall and my two thighs were hanging over the side of the bed, parted as much as possible. With eyes of fire, the prince gazed upon the delights spread before his view. Searing my mouth with burning kisses, he moved my hand away and placed his lance in, sliding it up and down very gently in the font. Roudolphine followed his slightest movement with eyes full of desire. Then he thrust his lance in as gently as possible. Up till then a very sweet sensation had penetrated me, but I had not felt any real delight. As he pressed, however, I was really being hurt and I began to moan.

Roudolphine encouraged me by sucking the tips of my breasts and fondling the place where the prince was trying to get it; she counselled me to arch my thighs upwards as much as possible. I obeyed automatically and the prince suddenly entered with such force that he penetrated halfway. I uttered a cry of pain and began to weep in earnest. I was lying there like a lamb at the sacrifice; however, I had made up my mind to go through with it. The prince moved slowly, this way and that, trying to penetrate further. I felt that all was not well; a muscle, a little skin, something anyway, had stopped him. Roudolphine had stuffed a handkerchief into my mouth to stifle my cries and I was now biting it in pain. I bore everything, however, to attain at last what I had desired so ardently.

Something wet was trickling down my thighs. Roudolphine cried out triumphantly. "Blood! It's blood! Congratulations, prince, on obtaining this beautiful virginity." The prince, who so far had proceeded as gently as possible, quite forgot himself and penetrated so vigorously that I felt his hairs entangled in mine. That did not hurt me too much, though, for the most painful part of the proceedings was over, but my expectations were not satisfied in the slightest. My conqueror became more passionate. Suddenly, I felt something hot flowing inside me, then the vigor relaxed and the member escaped. Really, I should be telling lies if I talked about pleasure. According to what Marguerite had told me, and according to my own experiments, I had been expecting something much greater than that. And I well remembered the enthusiasm my parents had shown too. At any rate, I was glad to see that my trick had succeeded and that I had not been wrong in my calculations.

As I lay there pretending to be unconscious I heard the prince talking enthusiastically about the visible signs of my virginity. My blood had, in fact, bespattered the bed and his dressing gown. This was far more than I had dared to hope for, especially after my wretched attempt with Marguerite's instrument; there was such a tremendous difference between that thing and the prince's mature virility! In any case, it was through no merit of mine that I had still been a virgin, but only through chance.

Virginity is actually a mythical thing anyway. I have often talked to other women about it and have heard the most contradictory statements. Some girls have so wide a membrane that there can be no obstacle to the first entry, while others have one so narrow that even after having several times participated in love bouts a man entering will still think that he is the first. In addition, it is very easy to deceive a man, especially if he believes that the girl is well behaved. This can be done by waiting until her period is about due before she surrenders, when she must moan a bit and twist around as if in pain, and the happy possessor swears that he has been the first, for a few drops of blood from a different source will easily mislead him.

But it was high time for me to awaken from my fainting fit. I had had my own way, and now I wanted to take pleasure without leaving my role of the seduced girl. The most important part had been acted. The prince and Roudolphine found particular delight in consoling me, for they were sure that they had initiated a novice. They both undressed and got into bed with me, the prince in the middle. The bed curtains were drawn and a delightful and indescribable game began. The prince was nice enough not to talk about love, langor or nostalgia. He was merely sensual, but with delicacy, for he knew that this quality is a spice to love play. I was still pretending that I had been violated, but that I was learning all the more quickly.

His two hands were busy with us, and ours with him. The more complicated our kisses became, the more animated our hands were and the more restless our bodies. Our nerves trembled with pleasure. It is a very great delight to kiss such a man, and he would have had to be made of stone not to warm up again. Even so, the second ejaculation had tired him. Sometimes he played with Roudolphine, sometimes with me, but I never let him approach without first having made his toilet, although he was very sure of himself. He gave me his word that I could try without a mask, that I risked nothing, that he was completely in control of himself. But I was not to be so easily tempted from the path I had chosen. So he began with Roudolphine, who lost consciousness two or three times without his strength being diminished. Then he washed and came to me. It still hurt a bit at first, but soon pleasure began to prevail, and for the first time I experienced complete fulfillment.

To prove to me once and for all that he was entirely master of his body, he did not finish inside me, but pulled out without ejaculating while I was half fainting with delight. He tore the condom wildly away and threw himself upon Roudolphine. She told me to come and sit upon her face and that she would calm with her tongue what the prince had brought to fever pitch. I was very reluctant, but a damp cloth refreshed the object of my desires and a charming group was soon composed. While the prince mounted Roudolphine, I knelt with my thighs wide apart over her face. Her tongue had plenty of room for its revels, for her head was thrown back over the pillows. Completely naked, because the prince had pulled off my nightdress in his passionate impatience, I was face to face with this magnificent man who now crushed my breasts against his chest and kissed me unceasingly.

Two tongues revived the fire which had hardly been extinguished. My pleasure increased and my kisses grew more and more passionate as I abandoned myself completely to this double excitement. The prince was enthralled, assuring us that he had never before experienced such happiness. At the moment of the spasm I grew jealous thinking of that warm wave of rapture spreading through Roudolphine and so, pretending to faint, I let myself fall heavily to one side. As I had calculated, I threw Roudolphine's cavalier right out of the saddle, and as I fell I saw their organs disunited where they had been so closely linked before. How fiery red and excited his was, how wide and violently open hers was. It was quite different from anything I had previously seen, though not more pleasant. I frightened them by falling, and they had no thought of pursuing their pleasures further, but came to help me.

I had reached my goal and was not long in coming to my senses. I made no secret of being very happy that I had been initiated with such art into the mysteries of love, but I refused to begin again as I could not stand any more. The prince wished to show u· that he could give up the greatest of pleasures if we could not all share it together. He said that he left it to us to content him. I did not know what he was expecting, but Roudolphine, more lascivious than ever, accepted at once. The prince lay back naked on the bed and I had to imitate Roudolphine, who provoked with her fingers the marvelous fountain. As I kissed him and played with the oval containers of his sweet balm, Roudolphine took the shaft in her mouth. Finally, the foamy jet sprang forth and fell upon us all. I would have liked to have taken the place of Roudolphine, who absorbed most of this burning fluid, but I still had to pretend to be inexperienced and just learning everything. You can understand why I cannot forget that incomparable night. The prince left us well before daybreak, and both Roudolphine and I, closely entwined, slept until after midday.

VIII

After this long and deep sleep, which permitted us to rest from the fatigues of the night, we had a copious breakfast. Over the meal Roudolphine had to make her confession, that is to say, she related in detail her affair with the prince. Fundamentally, her story was that of any sensual woman neglected by her husband. The prince, thanks to his wide experience, had very quickly realized the hidden unhappiness in Roudolphine's marriage, and she was not able to conceal her easily-awakened sensuality. In these circumstances, the prince had approached her prudently and adroitly. Passionate but outwardly cold, he was careful never to compromise himself. He had used the husband's flighty character as an excuse for Roudolphine's own unfaithfulness.

Roudolphine, a prey to her sensuality, and

having long desired to be revenged for her husband's coldness, had let herself be seduced. Usually vengeance is what most easily drives people into adultery, although married women will not willingly admit this. Roudolphine swore to me that she did not love the prince in the slightest, and yet I had ocassion to notice that she was jealous of his favors, if not of his friendship. She also declared to me that the prince was the only man to whom she had ever given herself apart from her husband.

I am perfectly willing to believe that. Roudolphine most jealously guarded her husband's reputation and her own honor, which were thus far absolutely blameless, and chose her acquaintances with the greatest care. Her husband would not have passively accepted any light behavior on his wife's part; even if he did not love her he had his pride and feared ridicule. Seeing this very special situation, I am prepared to believe that the prince really was the only man to whom she accorded her favors; on the other hand, I believe that I am right in thinking that before she met the prince she would probably have been an easy victim of any clever seducer if the greatest procuress—I mean, of course, opportunity—had been favorable to her.

Thus there was nothing unusual about Roudolphine's story. Stories such as these concerning my sex have always captivated me. Information of this sort interests me psychologically, for it widens my point of view and my knowledge of the world and people. It confirms my conception, which I have so often repeated, that our society lives on appearances, and that there are two kinds of morals: one for the world to see and the other for their private, lascivious behavior.

And indeed, how experienced I was in spite of my youth! First my grave, dignified father and my virtuous mother. Then there was Marguerite; although she was vivacious and animated, she always talked about what was "right," and "good behavior." She was continually lecturing my young cousin, yet what confessions she whispered into my young ear, and had I not seen with my own eyes how she appeased the desires that consumed her? Finally Roudolphine, this elegant young woman who gave herself to a man because conjugal joy was meted out too sparingly to suit her taste. And the prince; this man who appeared so cold, what a volcano of sensual vigor smoldered within him! Yet did these persons in their social circle not enjoy the reputation of the highest morality? Yes, I was right. Society is maintained entirely by appearances.

Now that I had attained my goal, that I was the confidante of Roudolphine and the prince, I thought my prudery out of keeping, and I admitted to Roudolphine, summoning up a blush, that the previous night's frolics and the prince's embraces had greatly delighted me. Roudolphine gave me a tender kiss in return for this avowal. She was still delighted to have been my mistress, and to have procured for me an enjoyment which in actual fact I owed only to my own cleverness.

That evening the prince did not leave us to pine in vain. He shared his caresses equally between Roudolphine and myself. My vanity told me that in spite of his apparent impartiality, he really preferred me strongly to Roudolphine. He was used to her and he found in me the attraction of novelty and change, which is, as you know, the spice of pleasure as much for men as for women. In any case, I did not take my vengeance yet. Roudolphine made the prince devote his first strength to her. The prince, to be just, did all he could to compensate me for this loss, but there is no point in giving you a detailed account of this night. I would only be repeating myself tiresomely. Given my preceding confessions, your imagination is quite capable of conjuring up the scenes that took place.

Unquestionably the first love of an inexperienced adolescent has an immense charm for any woman: to be his mistress, to lead him step by step, to initiate him into the sweet secrets of pleasure, and to show him the extent of its depths! The authority that a woman then exercises over a man flatters her vanity, and the ingenuous, rather clumsy caresses of a young man have their own peculiar charm. But it is only in the arms of an experienced man that a woman samples the most perfect sensual contentment. He must know all the secrets of pleasure and every means of renewing and increasing it. The prince was such a man. And if you remember that to this subtlety of the senses, and to his physical strength, were added the most perfect delicacy, that he was never brutal with the woman who surrendered to him, that he always seemed to have in mind only the woman's pleasure, thus making his own pleasure two-fold, you will soon have some idea what those unforgettable nights must have been like.

The following Sunday Roudolphine's husband arrived as usual. The prince was invited to dinner. In Vienna the prince was a frequent visitor at the banker's house; but in Baden he rarely appeared in Roudolphine's villa so as not to arouse suspicion.

Ever since I had become involved in their secret I had seen him only at night. Then, of course, no restraint had been imposed upon him because of the place, time and reason for our meetings. In spite of the strong control I exercised upon myself, as a rule, I must admit that when I saw the prince I could not still the violent beating of my heart. As he walked into the dining room I believe that my face reddened in a deep flush despite my efforts. The prince's behavior soon calmed me and helped me to pull myself together. He greeted Roudolphine with the familiarity which his dealings with her husband made permissible, but he saluted me ceremoniously and conventionally. At table, after the first few glasses of wine, he became silghtly more animated but without ever altering that coolness which was like second nature to him. Anyone who had seen us sitting at table would have had no reason to suspect the intimacy which existed between us. The prince's conduct was of a studied politeness no more, and aristocratically distant. He was a really superior example of his type of man, and he had a very wide scientific knowledge and great experience of the world and life in general. He was always perfectly composed, nothing ever embarrassed him, and it was always quite impossible to read his thoughts from his calm, impassive countenance. Courtly from head to foot, he was obliging and reserved, and yet his greatest quality was his discretion. He had had many successes with women, and he knew intimately all the subtle weaknesses of the human heart. He spoke rarely of his conquests and never mentioned names. A cold egoism, the fundamental trait of his character, permitted him to break off any affair which began to be tiresome, but no woman could ever complain of his unfaithfulness. He could break a woman's heart in cold blood, but he always spared her honor. Without love, and without need of tenderness, the prince sought only pleasure. That is why this man's friendship was so precious to me, for I too sought pleasure without wishing to give my heart.

Coffee was served in the garden. The prince offered his arm to Roudolphine, and the banker offered me his. As the two men moved away for a few moments to discuss some private affairs, Roudolphine expressed her regrets at her husband's return.

If Roudolphine intended to condemn me that night to continence, it did not fit in with my own intentions. As soon as the banker had arrived, I had made up my mind to have the prince to myself that night. I did not know how to signify to him that if Roudolphine had to give up any thought of seeing him then I was all the more anxious to see him myself. The prince, however, whispered in my ear that all I had to do was to give him the key to my bedroom. Half an hour later the key was in his hands.

The prince reached my room a little after midnight, and I spent a few wonderful hours in his arms. He assured me that he preferred me from every point of view to Roudolphine. The warmth of his kisses and the energy of his caresses were a proof that he was not merely trying to flatter my vanity. He was very excited and insatiable. In spite of all the pleasure he gave me, I was so exhausted that I fell asleep as soon as he left.

I did not wake up until Roudolphine came and shook me. At the first glance I saw that the prince had left his watch behind on the side of the hand basin. Roudolphine had seen it too; of course she realized at once the reason for my heavy slumber. She upbraided me violently for my fickleness, which might easily have compromised her in her husband's eyes. I told her calmly that I did not see how I could possibly have compromised her, since her husband, who had himself paid court to me, could hardly have reproached me for giving the prince every freedom. None of my arguments was successful in calming her. I realized that her bad temper was not so much dependent on fear of having been compromised as on jealousy. She envied the fervent embraces which had been given me since she had not been able to find compensation in the cold arms of her husband.

The following evening, when we were all three together again, it was obvious that my suspicions were right. Roudolphine did all she could to belittle me in the prince's eyes and tried to monopolize him. I found opportunity for revenge when Roudolphine had her period, which according to Jewish law banned all intercourse with men. The prince paid attention only to me, and this in Roudolphine's presence. This circumstance was the last straw. She was not in love with him, yet she felt insulted by this marked preference; and so I was not surprised to see her manner change and grow cooler.

One day she announced that family business obliged her to leave Baden earlier than usual. Thus she put an end to my liaison with the prince, but also broke off all relations with him herself, for she did not dare receive him in her Vienna house; it is quite true that jealousy and the need to suppress a rival will make one accept the most difficult sacrifices. Between ladies of high society, there is never any explanation of matters such as these, and so there was none between Roudolphine and myself. However, I did make her realize that I was aware that jealousy was the reason for her changed attitude. This remark did nothing to bring back our former feelings, and we, who had been inseparable, coldly took leave of each other. But is this not the case in all friendships between women?

With Roudolphine then, I returned to Vienna. As I visited her there but rarely, I hardly ever saw the prince. He had tried to approach me and had asked permission to come and see me, but I had to refuse him. I was too careful of my honor to risk compromising myself in such a way. In any case, even if I had desired to do so it would have been impossible for me to grant him a rendezvous, for my aunt supervised me very closely.

Thus it was that my liaison came to an end. Today I still remember with pleasure the handsome and clever prince, who was the first to teach me, not love, but the pleasure which a woman can feel in a man's embrace. Need I tell you, since you know me, that this rupture caused by Roudolphine's jealousy brought me the bitterest regrets? It was very hard for me to find someone else and I had to resume the very restricted joys of the hand. You know enough about the life of the theater to realize that I had no lack of admirers. A famous actress satisfies men's vanity, for they are happy to bathe in her reflected glory. Thus it is not surprising that a well-known artist should be surrounded by members of the oldest aristocracy and by financial tycoons. Even the most minor poet humbly brings her the first effusions of his muse. Adorers from all walks of society pursue her, all hang upon her glance, all thirst for her favors. But among all these men how was I to find the one I needed—someone who would be ready to satisfy all my desires without assuming any authority for himself? He had to be ready to be my slave, to see his affair with me come to an end at any moment, and I had to be able to rely upon his discretion. Only chance could help me to find such a man, and chance was by no means favorable.

I had a year's contract at the Kärntnertor Theater. It was drawing to an end, and when I was thinking of renewing it I was offered advantageous propositions from Budapest and Frankfurt. I liked Vienna, the lovely imperial city, and I should have preferred to stay there even for a less attractive salary. My father's fortunes had become rather shaky of late, however. For about a year I had been in no need of his help, but my gratitude towards him obliged me to help him now so far as I could. That is why I accepted the engagement in Frankfurt, where the best contract was offered. I said good-bye to Vienna.

I paid a very short farewell visit to Roudolphine. The pasage of time and her own jealousy had completely extinguished our friendship, which had been so charming in times past.

END OF PART I

PART II

I

You will be very surprised, my dear, to notice
how different the letters I am now going to send
you are from those I have written up to now.
Their style, conception, philosophy and viewpoint
have changed and the subjects will be much more
varied; however, I do not want you to think I
am tired of writing or that I have found a confidant to take up the composition of these
memoirs. If this were so, it would mean that I
had found a man in whom I could confide endless-
ly, as I can in you, but that is not the case. You
have to know men intimately, as I have been
fortunate to know you, to dare tell them everything you think and feel. Until now, I have not
met another one like that, especially among those
to whom I have given myself physically. The
change in my manner of writing comes from the
fact that I have changed my point of view while
relating my souvenirs. I live everything over
again as I go, as if I have been experiencing the
same emotions a second time, and perhaps I am
not wrong in adapting my style to suit each new
adventure.

I remember having seen in the prologue to
Goethe's *Faust* the following phrase, which I believe is an axiom, ". . . as rapid as the passage
from Good to Evil." This will show you how my
opinion of sensuality has changed. You will under-

stand this even better if you remember that fifteen months have passed since my last letter.

I told you at that time I accepted the engagement in Frankfurt because it was the most advantageous. It is fortunate that I only contracted to remain there two years, for from every point of view those were two years lost.

When I arrived in Frankfurt, Germany was not yet the prey of "Wagnermania," for Wagner was as yet unknown to the musical world; however, our repertoire was already in the worst possible taste. The struggle between German and Italian music was just beginning, and the German was beginning to triumph in Frankfurt.

A singer may love her homeland, she may cherish its language, its customs and the memories of her childhood, yet she has only one real homeland; the realm of music. And I have always preferred Italian music to any other. It conveys better our feelings and our soul, and it speaks the language of our heart better. It is more expressive, more passionate, more melting and sweeter than the erudite music of Germany or the light, brilliant music of France. The latter always seems to have been written for dancing the quadrille. Italian operas give the singers a chance to deliver everything of which they are capable, for it was written for them. German music is first and foremost instrumental and we always have to sacrifice ourselves in favor of the orchestra.

Besides, Frankfurt is the nastiest town I know. The aristocracy of money and Jews set the tone there, and nobody understands anything of art. People take a box at the opera just as they would go to a military parade. You are only important according to how much money you have. Art cannot flourish there; the strongest passion would freeze in that city. Love and pleasure are not a natural need, but "a refreshment to the spleen," as Shakespeare says.

I had plenty of admirers of many nationalities, but all their ancestors had crossed the Red Sea, and they surrounded me with respect when what I was thirsting for was sensuality. There was not a single one among them whom I thought worthy of my love and of the treasure which I carried incessantly within me. Among my colleagues there were a few good-looking, gallant men, but it is a principle of mine never to choose an actor, a singer or a musician. They are not nearly discreet enough; one's honor and sometimes one's contract is in danger with them, and I am particularly anxious to preserve the nimbus of virtue.

If only I had at least been able to meet a woman or a young girl! I would have given myself wholly as I had done to Marguerite, sparing nothing to reveal the sweet mysteries of love, but these people were always prudish, unapproachable, or very ugly. Others still were so practiced that they were worn out. They all filled me with horror and thus I was reduced once again to myself.

"And supposing I were to make the most of my forced stay in this boring town to strengthen myself and prepare myself for the love to come?" said I to myself often. "Am I incapable of doing that? And will future sensual pleasures compensate me for my chastity?" I decided to try. The wi'l of a human being is said to be the strongest thing in the world, and I submitted myself to the test.

During the first weeks I had tremendous difficulty in controlling myself. It cost me superhuman efforts to prevent my fingers straying of their own accord to a certain part of my body. As time went on, however, it became easier, and when dreams troubled me, when I was spurred on by the heat of my blood, I used to jump out of bed and either take a cold bath or open a newspaper to read a political article. Nothing cools me like reading about politics; by comparison even a cold shower is exciting.

After two months of voluntary mortification, the temptations became more rare, and when they did surprise me they were neither as intense nor as long lasting as they had been. I believe that I would have been able to give up love completely had I wanted to. That, however, is sheer folly and I do not know of any reason why I should have done it. One may be chaste in order to experience later a pleasure all the stronger. Chastity is then a stimulant. When you intend to go to a ball you do not tire yourself out by taking long walks just beforehand, and when you are invited to a succulent dinner you do not fill your stomach just before going to it. It is the same with the pleasures of love.

Yet I do not know whether I should ordinarily have been able to stand that sort of life for two years! I believe that I owe it to divine chance that I got through the test at all.

I can imagine you smiling, for you do not believe what I have said. Just listen, then, for I swear that I am writing you the pure truth. One of my colleagues, Madame Denise, a Frenchwoman by birth, but who spoke perfect German, was the only one among all the singers with whom I could speak freely on any subject. Her influence was so great that I had nothing to fear in connection with her discretion. She had known everything; her experience was immense. She was too blasé to be subject to sexual itchings, but not old nor ugly enough to be unable to find cavaliers. And if she allowed this one and that one to pay court to her, it was in order to get everything she could from them, as is done in Paris.

Some people whose bizarre taste drew them towards Denise had come to me to ask me to act as intermediary, and I was good-natured enough to attempt to intercede on their behalf. That is how our friendship grew up.

"I have lost all desire for pleasure, not because I am already exhausted, but through sheer disgust," she said. "When you think, when you read to what extremes that sort of pleasure can drag you, you do not want it any more. The water is cool, then lukewarm, then boiling. You fall into a mud pit to disappear. You will soon learn about it if you tread that path.

"I was once married to the worst rake you can imagine. His debauchery finally even killed him. It was a terrible sickness, for several diseases were gnawing at him while he was still alive. Although he died of tuberculosis of the spine, he also had syphilis, his body was one huge sore, and he went blind. He was not yet thirty-three years old when he died. I adored him and was desperate at having lost him. He used to go to the Bois de Boulogne every day, but in less than six months he was unable to move. I looked after him with one of my friends; we had to do everything for him, as for a babe in arms.

"Do you know to whom he owed such a frightful end? To an infamous individual, a Monsieur Duvalin, who called himself his friend.

"When I reproached Duvalin and accused him of being my husband's murderer, he shrugged his shoulders and told me that it had not been his intention to cause his downfall but, on the contrary, that he had wanted to warn him against his evil inclinations. He said it was not his fault if his remedy had been unsuccessful."

" 'What can I say, Madame?' Duvalin had asked. 'I too have been tortured by the demon of the flesh, but by reading that book which killed your husband I was cured of every natural desire. I do not say that I have become an ascetic, but at least I no longer belong to Epicurus' herd of pigs, they who made a mud pit of sexual love. Disgust disenchanted me; mud attracted him. Which of us was at fault?'

"In my despair I wanted to kill myself," Mme. Denise continued, "but I wanted to do it bizarrely because I was naturally of a fantastic turn of mind. My husband, during our marriage, had exhausted every kind of animal pleasure that you can experience with one woman. I wanted to die of debauchery like my husband. Thus Hindu women mount the funeral pyre after their husband's death and let themselves be consumed alive by the flames.

"There was no end to my love," she added. "The death I was choosing had been his, and I assure you that it would have been much more torturing than any death by fire. I wanted to study the theory of animal sensuality, then apply it to practice. My husband had made me the gift of a few of the works on the subject, for example, *The Memoirs of Fanny Hill, Little Escapades,*

The Story of Dom Bougre, The Cabinet of Love and of Venus, The Indiscreet Jewels, Voltaire's *The Maid* and *The Cauchois Lady.*

"He had read part of them to me in times past to put us both in the mood for pleasure, and had always succeeded, finding me ready for all the filthiness he desired. After his death, I came across de Sade's book at the back of a double-floored cupboard and I began to read it. My impatience forced me to explore the meanings of the illustrations. I read the text preceding the most frightful pictures; for example, the woman being tortured, the scene in the menagerie, the adventure on Etna, the flagellations, the rape of small boys, the scenes in Rome, the one in which the Marquis de Sade dressed in a leopard skin hurls himself among naked women and children and bites a little boy to death, and finally the description of the orgies where two women are guillotined, the bestialities occur, *etcetera*.

"Now I was beginning to understand Duvalin. The book could have a double influence according to the temperament of the reader, according to how sensitive he or she happened to be, and what sort of mind he had. Duvalin was blasé about it; but myself, I was seized with disgust and horror and it cost me so much effort to finish reading it that I was already incapable of all feeling before proceeding to the practice. I could caress myself as much as I liked, but when I took my finger away the sensation was dull and empty. The backbone of sex was broken for me and I had no desire to indulge in it again. I was cured in one stroke of any voluptuous itching which may exist in the human body. I was beginning to understand the state of mind of a eunuch."

Denise told me much more on the same subject. She thought that I was completely inexperienced as far as practice was concerned. She suspected that I was familiar with manual satisfaction, or the pleasure which an instrument such as Marguerite's can procure, or even embraces between persons of my own sex; but she thought that I was completely ignorant of men. Pretence is innate in women, just as boastfulness is in men. She asked me whether I had read any of the books she had mentioned, and on my negative reply she advised me to begin at once with *Justine and Juliette*.

"Some doctors claim," she said, "that camphor has the property of extinguishing the sexual urge of a woman."

I do not know if that is true or not, but Sade's book stifled for three whole months every thought or desire for sensuality and debauchery. What an imagination! Is it possible that such things should happen? In this book men are tigers and hyenas, women are snakes and alligators. What you find least in it is natural sexuality. Women make love with women, men with boys and animals. It is horrible! I wondered if it were possible that a man should ever satiate himself. Or that he should have recourse to such means of excitement, that he should desire tortured, burned, torn bodies instead of beautiful white ones. I was afraid of the man who had written that. Had he really led such a life, or was it his distorted imagination which made him write such things? He says somewhere that these were the customs of the knights of his time and that similar scenes took place in the Parc-aux-Cerfs.

He talks of the pleasure of watching men die,

mentioning that the famous Marquise de Brinvilliers undressed her victims and took delight in the shudders and the contortions of the naked bodies of these unfortunate wretches. During the whole time I was reading this, which was several months, I did not think even once of doing again what I had done with Marguerite and with Roudolphine. It took me a long time to read ten volumes of three hundred pages each, especially since I could not devote all my leisure time to them; I had to study new scores; every day there were rehearsals or performances; I entertained and visited a lot; I was invited to balls, evening parties, pleasure parties in the country, *etcetera*. Besides that, I did not know French well enough to be able to understand exactly what Sade wrote. Many words escaped me and I could not find them in any dictionary.

Thus I spent two years living as chastely as Saint Mary Magdalene who, by the way, also had a very troubled, stormy youth.

Towards the end of the second year I received several offers of contracts from different theaters in Germany, Austria and Hungary. I was having some difficulty in making up my mind when two gentlemen arrived; one named Monsieur de R. was very handsome and very wealthy on his own account and a great dilettante of music. He promptly began to pay court to me and promised me a much more handsome income than the others could offer as theater managers. Had I accepted, I should have lowered myself in my own esteem. I would have found it repulsive to sell my favors to Mammon, and so I refused his offers.

The other gentleman was the manager's son, a young man of barely nineteen years, good-looking, shy, and as timid as a little peasant boy. He hardly dared to look at me and if I spoke to him he blushed as red as a peony. The Baron of O. spoke very well of him, telling me that he was a genius and would one day play a great role in his homeland. Really it was worthwhile receiving the first love of such a young man. If ever a person were unaware of the theory, of the practice, of the sweet secrets of Cytherea, it was indeed young Arpard de H. son of the Hungarian manager's sister! The gentlemen were only staying two days in Frankfurt; they were on their way to London and Paris to buy some operas then fashionable. Monsieur de R. pressed me to accept, the Baron of O. added his entreaties to those of the manager, and I read in the eyes of Arpard his desire that I accept. This glance decided me. The manager immediately drew out a contract in duplicate, read it to me, and I set my signature to it. I was engaged to sing in Budapest as soon as my Frankfurt contract terminated. I was, however, authorized to give six gala performances in Vienna. I was to begin just at the off-season.

I left Frankfurt in July. Before going there I had had photographs done by Angerer, but I no longer looked anything like those photographs. My features were more strongly marked, I appeared younger than I was in reality. Doctors, and men and women among my friends, have often told me that I was very well developed for my age. I remember very well what my mother looked like when I discovered her in bed on my father's birthday. What a difference there was between her and me at that time! My thighs were then not as thick and fleshy as her arms. Her bones were not the slightest bit in evidence, but mine protruded everywhere — shoulders, shoulder blades, hips; you could even see my ribs. During the two years in which I had been living the life of a Vestal Virgin, I had put on some weight. The thighs and the two spheres of Venus, which are the special pride of a woman, had become rounded; they were firm and yet soft; I never tired of looking at myself in the mirror and wished I had been as supple as a serpent so that I could have twisted myself round to kiss these fair globes.

The scenes of flagellation in Sade's book had made me curious about what pleasure one could procure from whipping one's behind. One day I took a willow rod, undressed, and planted myself before the mirror to try. The first blow hurt me so much that I stopped at once. I was as yet unaware that you had to begin by slaps as light as those administered by the masseuses in Turkish baths, and that it is only at the moment of the spasm that you strike with all the strength in your arm. Several years passed before I knew this pleasure. If the pain had not discouraged me I should surely have resumed the play of my fingers in spite of my firm principles of chastity. Besides, every time I took a bath, which occurred three or four times a day in the summer, I was on the point of yielding to the temptations of Denise's book which chilled me.

When I passed through Vienna, all my acquaintances were surprised by the change in my physical appearance. I had arranged to meet my mother, who was to be present at my triumph. As soon as she saw me she threw her arms about me saying, "My dear child, how lovely you are, and how well you look."

Once I ran into Roudolphine at Dommaier's in Hitzing. She too had changed, but not for the better. She rouged her cheeks to conceal how pale she was, but could not hide the dark rings around her eyes.

"Have you given up the pleasures of love since you left Vienna?" she asked me. "But that is impossible, for anyone who has tasted of that ambrosia can never do without it. There are some people who bloom with the pleasures of love instead of fading, and you are among them!"

In vain I swore to her that for two years I had led the life of a recluse and that my health was all the better for it. She would not believe me, saying that it was absurd.

"Whom could I have found in Frankfurt?" I asked her. "Students? They are the very antidote of love. They have no idea of gallantry. It is unworthy of a woman to give herself to a man who can have absolutely no place in her heart. Nothing horrifies me more than Messalina, who sought for nothing but animal sensuality."

Roudolphine blushed under her paint; I had probably touched the right spot, although quite involuntarily. I noticed two horsemen who were staring at us through their lorgnettes; one of them saluted Roudolphine while I left by another path.

During the two weeks I stayed in Vienna, I learned that Roudolphine was considered one of the most flirtatious women in society. Her lovers could be counted by the dozens. The two gentlemen whom I had noticed at Hitzing were among them; they were attached to the Brazilian embassy and were the greatest rakes in Vienna. Roudolphine actually introduced one of them to me. She was no longer jealous; on the contrary, she willingly passed on her lovers to her friends. She confided to me that she felt almost as much pleasure in watching the sensual joys of others. I thought of the scenes in *Justine*, where something similar happens.

Out of politeness, I went to visit Roudolphine, one afternoon, finding her alone. She showed me some photographs she had just received from Paris. They were erotic scenes, naked men and women. The most interesting were those of Madame Dudevant, which Alfred de Musset was circulating among his friends.

There were six others which were particularly obscene. The famous woman of letters was initiating women and young girls to the mysteries of the service of Sappho. In one of these pictures she was making love with an enormous gorilla, in another with a Newfoundland dog, in yet another with a stallion that two girls were holding in rein. She herself was on her knees, her buttocks appearing in all their splendor; underneath, the grotto was wide open to let the terrible lance of the stallion penetrate as he pushed painfully. I cannot believe that a woman can bear such mastery from such a quarter. The pain must be much greater than the pleasure.

Roudolphine told me the story of these pictures. You do not know about it, perhaps, and I think it is interesting enough to be worthwhile relating.

George Sand lived very intimately for several years with Alfred de Musset. They traveled together in Italy until in Rome, after a terrible scene of jealousy, they broke completely. Musset was extremely discreet and respected her rather as his lover than as a woman. George Sand, on the other hand, went around saying she had dropped the poet on account of his weakness in the tourneys of love, and that he was quite impotent. These falsehoods came to Musset's ears, and his vanity was wounded by them, for he was losing his prestige with all women. He wanted to revenge himself, so he had these photographs made, adding to them a scandalous text in verse. These pictures had been circulated in photograph form because he had not been able to find a printer willing to understake even their private publication.

I was very happy to be reconciled with Roudolphine; yet her visits embarrassed me because she had such a bad reputation. I was impatient to get to Budapest and once my performances were over I did not lose a single day.

I arrived there during the great annual fair, which is the liveliest period in the off-season. The fair lasts two weeks and is called the St. John's Market, or the Melon Market, for at this time the market is full of that succulent fruit.

I had provided myself with a Hungarian-German vocabulary and a manual of the Magyar language. When I arrived in Budapest I immediately sent my card to Monsieur de R., who was kind enough to come and visit me at once. He was accompanied by his nephew Arpard, and the adolescent's eyes shone with pleasure when he saw me.

I was very surprised to see these two gentlemen enter in Hungarian national costume and I only found out later that this was the fashion at the time. Monsieur de R. invited me to dress in the national costume myself. This nationalistic fad was so strong that persons who opposed it were insulted on the streets by many of the younger folk. As a member of the national theater, it would particularly be expected of me to conform — a thing I found abusive, for there was no word of it in my contract. However, as this costume suited me very well, I did adopt it and I looked much prettier than in my town clothes. I had several costumes made and wore them in preference to all others.

Monsieur de R. asked me whether I preferred to sing in Italian or German. I realized that he really wanted to ask me another question, so I replied that I would do my best to learn enough Hungarian to be able to sing in that language. As speech is used only rarely in opera and as the audience never understands the text you are singing anyway, I thought that it would not be too difficult. I added that I would take lessons.

Monsieur de R. recommended to me a lady of the theater who spoke German well and who gave lessons.

It is custom in Hungary to feast visitors at any hour of the day. In a general way, eating is one of the principal occupations of the Hungarians; they are great voluptuaries. So I invited the two gentlemen to take some refreshment. Monsieur de R. excused himself, saying he had a lot to do and got up to leave. "If you would like to stay," he said to his nephew, "I will permit you to accept the young lady's invitation. Afterwards you could show her the city and act as her guide."

I was very pleased to find myself alone with Arpard, for I had decided to teach him the art of love and to start by bending him to my caprices.

II

I made up my mind to bewitch Arpard, but I did not quite know how to set about it. I should have had no difficulty in seducing him, but I had to be careful of so many things and I only fully realized the danger when Monsieur de R. had left us alone together. Arpard was so very young and I knew that once I had allowed him to possess me, it would no longer be possible to hold him back. I was well aware that this young man was not like my accompanist Franz, to whom I could say "so far and no further," who was a man made for servitude and obedience and as well trained as my aunt's dog. Some mischance might come about and I would be risking everything by making a mistake at the beginning of my new engagement. In any case, I did not know enough about Arpard and could not be certain of his discretion.

Young men are inclined to be boastful about their conquests. And even if they do not boast of them they are apt to give themselves away by a glance or through some hasty word. Besides, we might easily be caught.

If I had known Hungarians then as well as I was to know them later, I would not have been quite so hesitant, but I had just arrived from Frankfurt, where a woman's conduct was very severely judged. My heart was thumping so hard when Monsieur de R. left me alone with his nephew that I could hardly speak. I was aware by this time that I was completely infatuated with him. Oh, if only I could have communicated to him the feelings which swept through me, for it was not merely sensual desire; it was that ethereal love which I had read about. I could have spent hours just looking at him and listening to the sound of his voice, and I would have been unspeakably happy.

When Monsieur de R. had gone, the butler of the *Hotel de la Reine d'Angleterre* where I was staying brought in the refreshments I had ordered, consisting of coffee, cream, ices, nut tarts, assorted fruits — especially melons — and iced punch. He brought us only refreshing things. Arpard sat down beside me and, as it was very hot, I took off the silk fichu which covered my neck and bosom, confronting Arpard with my twin, milky white peaks. At first he only peeked at them out of the corner of his eyes, but when he saw that I obviously did not mind this liberty, he leaned towards me slightly and went on staring. He was suffering and his voice trembled.

As I handed him a glass of iced coffee, I brushed against his hand and our fingers touched for a second. I felt the moment of my defeat approaching and struggled, but weakly, against it. A little shiver ran over my body, I became suddenly dreamy, and our conversation lagged abruptly. I leaned back on the sofa; my eyes were closed, my brain was reeling, and I felt as if I were going to faint. I must have changed color, for Arpard asked me in a worried tone if I felt ill. I pulled myself together and thanked him with a handclasp, over which we lingered, for his concern. I then let him take my left hand, and he covered it with kisses. His face was scarlet, and his bosom swelled so much that I thought all his coat buttons would burst.

How much longer were these preliminaries going to last? He was much too shy to make the most of the advantages he had; indeed, he was not even aware of having any advantage. Any rake would have used the opportunity at once. I would have done all I could to have hidden my feelings. The situation was growing painful, and I reminded Arpard that his uncle had asked him to visit the town with me. I rang and asked for a cab to be sent.

"The Baron of O.'s carriage is below," the servant answered. "It is at your disposal."

This was most courteous, especially as I had not yet seen the baron and had forgotten to send him my card. I decided to deliver it to him at once, so we went to his house. Unfortunately he was not in, and we continued our ride as far as Ofen. Then we returned over the same route through the little forest outside the town. It was a sort of park in very bad taste, with a small lake dotted with boats. I asked Arpard if we were very far from my hotel, and he said it was about an hour's walk away. "I'll send away the carriage and we can take a little stroll here. Do you think you will be too tired?" he asked.

"Even if it lasts until tomorrow morning I shall not be tired in the slightest." He smiled, thinking of another sort of tiredness.

The people of Budapest only visit this park during the day, and as soon as the sun goes down they all return to town. I was in no hurry to go back though, for Budapest is the dustiest city I know. All the surrounding countryside is nothing but a great waste of sand where every gust of wind raises clouds of dust. I was glad to be sheltered from it and to be strolling across the grass. We crossed over onto the islands by the suspension bridges, I hanging all the while on Arpard's arm. He led me into a restaurant which was still open. I asked what time it closed and was told at nine, and that it reopened at four o'clock in the morning. Arpard, meanwhile, pressed me to go home soon because the wood was not a safe place in the evening, and someone had recently been killed there.

"But surely you are not afraid, my dear Arpard?" I asked him, for we were already calling each other by our first names. Our familiarity had made great progress, chiefly because I had obliged him to declare his love for me. He swore to me by the stars to love me until he died, saying that he had first fallen in love in Frankfurt. His imagination was ardent and poetic like that of all young people. He pressed my hands between his own and kissed them, and when we arrived on one of the islands he fell at my feet, saying he adored the very ground I walked on, and begging me to let him kiss my feet. I leaned towards him and kissed his hair, his forehead, his eyes. He took me by the waist and buried his head — you cannot guess where? — in the area of that place which all men seek. Even though it was well concealed by my clothes, hidden beneath the layers of my dress and petticoats, Arpard seemed intoxicated by its presence. He took my hand and pressed it against his heart, beneath his vest. It was galloping and pounding as strongly as mine.

Meanwhile, one of my knees slid against his legs and touched something hard which, at that contact, became harder and larger yet. I thought that his trousers would split. It was eleven o'clock, we were still on the little island, and we were now wrapped tightly in each other's arms. My legs were pressed against his knees and he finally dared to lift the hem of my dress. He first played with the laces of my boots, then began to climb higher until he was all the way to my garters. His hand finally touched and caressed my bare thighs. At that caress I was already beside myself with ecstasy, and our mouths joined, my lips sucking his, my tongue searching for his. I wished to swallow him whole, so much did I hunger.

I still do not know how it happened, but suddenly I found his scepter in my hands. I manipulated it as if to rend it completely from him, while his right hand reached my warm, moist front. Although it was instinct rather than experience that guided him, he tickled me and thrilled me until I thought I would go crazy. His thumb and index finger played at the top, while his other three fingers found the entrance completely open and waiting further down. My interior burned as if filled with boiling lava and I was nearly fainting, the thrill and shiver raced through me so. I lowered my eyes and saw his superb rod as large and rearing as the horn of a fighting bull.

Though I had not yet touched it, its nude head was fiery and purple. I slid my hand down to it and felt it shiver. An electric discharge filled the palm of my hand, gushing like a jet of water from his source of life, and my open mouth drank deeply of everything his loins could give. At the same instant, I felt my own fountain overflow. His hands were filled as if he had dipped them into a crystal well, and he lifted them to his mouth and drank their contents, licking his palms and even running his tongue between his fingers. Since no one had taught him these things, he let nature drive him, and he followed its inspirations.

Even after this double ecstasy he was not at all weakened or enervated and, like me, desired still more pleasure. As we lay thinking for a second how we would resume our delights, my reason began to whisper to me that dishonor was awaiting me, that I was going to become pregnant, and that I was going to have a child and die, but my fiery lover resumed his attack at that moment, and even if a group of strangers had seen us and come to mock me, I would have continued that game of love and cried aloud my happiness. I would not have felt the slightest shame; I was a complete slave to my desire.

The ecstasy lasted several minutes, and even after the reciprocal spurting of our nectars once more, my fire again became more ardent each second, and Arpard was in the same state. My eyes traveled from his face to his proud spur to the dark and silent landscape around us; they wandered across the surface of the nearby pool, scarcely marred by a few rare plants. The moon threw its reflection across the water, which occasionally burst into tiny ripples when some small fish leaped after a night-flying insect. I suddenly wanted to dive into this tiny lake and take a refreshing bath.

Arpard guessed my thoughts and whispered in my ear, "Would you like to swim with me? There isn't the slightest danger. Everyone is asleep at the restaurant, and there isn't a soul about."

"But you told me that this wood is dangerous, that someone was killed here at night. Even so, I *would* like to do it."

"Do not worry, my dear angel. This part is

much safer than any other," he said softly.

"But what will people say at the hotel if we come home so late?"

"The hotel stays open all night, and the porter sleeps in his office. You know the number of your room, and the chambermaid will surely have left the key in the door. In any case, it is not hard to find an excuse. I often take a room in that hotel myself when I do not want to wake up my uncle's janitor. I just take the first key I come across, and it is almost like being at home. Your neighbor left today, so that room is empty and I will take it."

"Since you are so reassuring, I will try it. Help me to undress."

He promptly threw off his Hungarian cap and his braided leather jacket, and helped me to unfasten my corset. In less than three minutes, we both stood naked in the moonlight.

Arpard had never seen a woman naked before and all his limbs were trembling. He knelt down before me and kissed every part of my body from head to foot, back and front. He sucked the tips of my breasts, kissed the temple of pleasure, passed his tongue between the great lips, and caressed me as deeply as he could penetrate. At last, I escaped from him and jumped into the water. I swam away vigorously, but Arpard soon caught up and began swimming with one hand while with the other he clasped me. From time to time he dived under the surface, his curly head brushing against my breasts and over my stomach. Then he caressed the center of my pleasure now with his fingers, now with his tongue. Soon our feet touched bottom where the water was more shallow, and our desires threw us into each other's arms and I received that dispenser of joys which can sometimes be such a devastator.

Not for a moment did I think of the possible consequences of my abandon. If I had seen a dagger between his hands, I would have presented my breast for him to strike. But as he was inexperienced his spasm was there before he had driven in his shaft, the horn of plenty emptied itself, and the precious juice ran down my legs. But he was not discouraged. He clasped me closer, breathing heavily, and his fingers dug into my flesh. His wand hung lifeless only for a moment, then it rose again and I could feel it growing, hardening and heating. Suddenly, with one energetic thrust, he buried it to the depths. It would have been painful if it had not been so exquisite. I felt certain now that I would become pregnant. But a shiver ran across my limbs, starting first in my loins and racing down to my toes. My lock gates were open wide and the floods rushed out so impetuously that he thought, as he told me later, that I was splashing him with something else. This excited the same canal in him and I felt a burning flow penetrate me that I thought would never stop. It was certainly not the juice of his loins, for after the last drop he continued to ravage my interior although it was long since dry. We were tightly pressed to each other and incapable of saying a single word, not a thought in our heads, lost in a deep dream of love. I would have liked to stay like that forever.

The sound of the church bells of Saint Theresa were carried to us on the winds: midnight was striking. I told Arpard it was time to go back to town and that we could resume our lovemaking at the hotel. He obeyed and asked if I would let him carry me in his arms like a child as far as the edge of the pool. He clasped his hands beneath me, I put mine together around his neck, and he carried me as far as the bench, where our clothes were. I put on my stockings and he laced up my shoes for me, kissing my knees and my calves as he did so. At last we finished and went off in the direction of the crossroads.

On the drive at the edge of the wood, a cab was standing. The driver was sitting on the seat, and Arpard asked him to take us into town immediately, directing him to Saint Joseph's Square. He wanted to conceal from him my identity and my residence. I too had become prudent and pulled my veil over my face. The coachman accepted a silver florin and we started off at a gallop. We got out at Saint Joseph's Square, from where it was not far to my hotel. I went in first while he disappeared to get the keys, and waited outside the door. He was there within a few minutes and told me that the porter was asleep and that no one had seen us enter. I felt tired, my legs ached after having made love standing, and I really wanted to sleep. So I went to bed at once. Arpard seemed tired too. His spring had gushed forth three times, and I advised him to try to regain his strength by going to bed at once. He would have liked to have stayed with me, but he had enough delicacy to leave me after kissing me passionately once more.

I am not going to tell you about all of our lovemaking. With this conquest of Cytherea's realm, I would have to plagiarize and repeat myself and it would only bore you. Arpard admitted that in Frankfurt he had purchased the *Memoires of Monsieur de H.*, from which he had learned the theories of the pleasures of love. He also told me that several times he had been on the point of bringing his first fruits to a prostitute, that only the fear of infection had prevented it, and that it was to his great good fortune that I had come to Hungary.

On that first evening I had neglected all the precautionary measures which I usually insisted on. Later, I had recourse to these measures of prudence again. I wanted to make certain that there should be no nasty surprises in store for me. Even so, however, I did sometimes neglect them, but no ill consequences befell our relationship. Since you are a doctor, you can easily explain this phenomenon.

My happiness was not to last long. In October Arpard was given work to do a long way from Budapest and had to leave. His parents lived in this part of the country, and his father was such a severe man that Arpard did not dare go against his will.

In September I rented an apartment in Hatvner Street in the house of the Horvat family. I did not do my own cooking, but had many meals brought from the casino. It was much more profitable to me, for I had no need to invite my colleagues to dinner as I would have had to do if I had had a home of my own, for Hungarians are very hospitable. The actors and actresses and singers invited each other in turn and sponged on one another.

I engaged a teacher of Hungarian, an actress who was recommended to me by the baron. He advised me not to take the one that Monsieur de R. had recommended, for she had a bad reputation in the city.

Madame de B., my Hungarian teacher, had been very beautiful in her youth. She had had a rather eventful life; her husband was a drunkard and she had divorced him. She spoke German very well and had only learned Hungarian in order to be able to take up the theater. Her father had been a civil servant and she had had a very good education. She paid me the compliment of saying that she had never yet met anyone who learned Hungarian as easily as I did.

We soon became as good friends as if we had been of the same age. She made no secret of her adventures and often talked to me about them. She had not had many lovers, yet she knew every shade of sexual pleasure as well as Messalina. I could not hide my astonishment.

"You see," she said, "I had women friends who felt no embarrassment in engaging in front of me in all sorts of filth, so I learned about it all by being present without ever taking part. Madame de L., whom Monsieur de R. recommended to you, was the most dissolute of all when she was young, and she would be now if she were not so old. However, she still has two or three men who give her love's service. I have heard of Messalina, Agrippina, Cleopatra, and other wanton women, but I would not be able to believe in the stories told of them, if I had never known Madame de L. You ought to get to know her, for she knows all the procuresses in Budapest and is in contact with all the prostitutes. She could teach you things of which most women are usually quite unaware."

I ought to point out to you that I had talked to Madame de B. about the book by the Marquis de Sade, and that I had shown her the pictures. She had never seen them before, but she told me that she was sure Madame de L. probably knew of them, for she had seen her doing the very same things.

"What would you be risking if you too were to see those things?" she said in response to my question. "No one would ever find out. I can assure you that Anna (that was Madame de L.'s first name) is discretion personified. You get a certain amount of pleasure from being present at these spectacles, for it gives you a chance to know men in their moral undress. And you would not believe how many of the most important ladies of Budapest indulge in excesses of this sort! They are worse than prostitutes and no one suspects them. Anna knows them all for she has seen them all when they thought they were safe from curious eyes. And not just with one man either, but with half a dozen."

Madame de B. had whetted my curiosity. The scenes of *Justine and Juliette* simply disgusted me. I would never have wanted to be present, for example, at what takes place in volume eight, page three, or in volume ten, page ninety. Yet there were some things which I felt I would have been able to stand.

You probably know the marquis' book and you know what the pictures are about, but if you do not remember them let me describe them to you. The first one represents an arena. At the top you can see at a window an old man with a beard who is the proprietor of the menagerie. Then a young man, a girl barely of marriageable age, and a little boy. A naked girl is just being thrown out of the window. There is a lion in the act of devouring another girl, whose intestines are hanging out of her body. An enormous bear is sniffing at a third girl. Even you, a doctor, and used to being present at the most terrible operations, must be horrified by this picture. You can imagine how I felt, then!

The second picture shows the Marquis de Sade. He is dressed in a panther skin and is attacking three naked women. He has his arm around one already and is biting her chest while blood flows from the wound. His right hand is tearing her other breast. On the ground lies a child, naked, torn and bitten to death.

I do not know which is the more terrible of these two images. I should not like to be present at any scenes such as these, but there are others, orgies, torture scenes and debauchery between persons of the same sex, which one could watch.

You will perhaps say that the most innocent scenes may lead to the most cruel. I do not claim that there are not certain natures which know no limits, but I can assure you that such will never be my case. You might just as easily say that every person who is present at executions or corporal punishment — it is known that there are always many more women than men — would be capable of murdering his fellow humans to satisfy his morbid desires, if he were not afraid of punishment. But I am sure this is wrong. One of my friends, a Hungarian woman, whose father was an army officer and lived with his family in the Asler barracks at Vienna, was present nearly every day at corporal punishments. Through her windows she saw how soldiers were beaten with rods and flails in the courtyard, yet she never had the slightest desire to do anything like that to anyone in the world; she wasn't even capable of cutting a chicken's neck. There is a huge gulf between participation and attendance, I think.

Madame de L. visited in the best families of Budapest. Ladies of the highest society were her intimate friends, and she most likely gave them lessons in the art which she understands so well, that of attracting men. There was nothing compromising in getting to know her, although in Germany there would have been, so I agreed to receive her, and Madame de B. brought her to me. Only the baron appeared displeased and said this was no company for me to keep. I do not know why he detested her so much, for I liked her quite well. There was nothing provocative about her, or at least I thought not. When we knew each other better and I had asked her to tell me all, she threw off all restraint, and I suddenly realized that this woman really was quite different from what she seemed to be in company. She had a strange philosophy which was concerned only with finding ever-renewed means for satisfying the senses. She was a sort of female Sade and would have been capable of doing everything that was mentioned in the book. I soon had proof of that, as I shall tell you. We were talking of the ways in which the sexual pleasure of a man and a woman can be enlivened, since the sensitiveness of the sexual organs is worn down as time passes and artificial means must be resorted to in order to revive it.

"I shall never advise any man to do all the things I have done," she said. "There is nothing more dangerous than too much excitement for a man. He gets overwrought and it makes him impotent. Imagination is a bad and rare substitute for what he has squandered. In a woman, on the other hand, the imagination increases the excitement and the pleasure. Have you ever tried having yourself lightly whipped with rods while you were making love?"

I must say now that with Madame de L. it was pointless to tell lies. From her first visit she recognized to what degree I had been initiated into the mysteries of love, but I had nothing to fear, for she agreed with my opinions concerning the secrecy of these things and the dissimulation innate to women. So I told her that I had tried once but that it had hurt so much that I had given up, and she burst out laughing.

"There are very few women who are familiar with the pleasure of pain, especially with rods or a whip," she said. "Among the many women prisoners who are condemned to be lashed, there is scarcely one who would not be afraid of it and, up to now, I have only met two girls who appreciate this sort of pleasure. One was a prostitute from Raab; she committed several thefts merely in order to be whipped, and her pleasure was increased all the more at being punished in public. She was very proud of being called a whore. When the blows fell upon her she screamed and wept, but as soon as she got back in her cell she undressed, looked in the mirror at her back covered with horrible marks, while her fingers played in her shell. During the punishment, even in the midst of the keenest pain, she had the most voluptuous flows. I have just discovered the other girl here in the city. She is in the city prison and gets thirty lashes every three months. She never makes a fuss, and her facial expression shows more pleasure than pain. Would you like to be there when her punishment is carried out?"

I hesitated, for I was afraid that Monsieur de

F., the governor of the city, would find out about it. I knew him well, for he was one of my admirers. Anna — I am calling her Anna since that was what Madame de B. called her — assured me that Monsieur de F. would never find out and that Madame de B. and other ladies would be present, among them some members of the highest aristocracy, so that I could easily pass unnoticed, and that if I were well veiled nobody would recognize me.

In the end, I agreed; the day was near when the prisoner was to be punished, so I did not have long to wait.

On the appointed day, there was yet another spectacle which prevented all the ladies of the aristocracy from coming. So, Anna, Madame de B. and I stealthily entered a room prepared for us, and settled ourselves before the window. Soon three men appeared: the militia chief, a prison warder and the guard. The delinquent was a girl of between sixteen and eighteen years, beautiful as a young goddess, gracefully built and with a face shining with innocence. She was not afraid, but she turned her eyes away when she saw us. The warder tied her on a bench and the guard whipped her with a rod. She was wearing only a very thin petticoat and her chemise, which were stretched tightly across her body so that one could see the roundness of her form. Her buttocks trembled with every blow and she was biting her lips, but even so her face betrayed her pleasure. At the twentieth blow her mouth opened, uttered a sigh; she seemed to be enjoying the greatest ecstasy.

"This ought to have happened either much earlier or much later," whispered Anna to me.

"I don't think she will reach the ecstasy a second time. We shall have to procure it for her when she comes back here after her punishment. I have given the warder five florins to let her come in here . . . I did it for you."

I realized what she meant, and gave her ten florins to cover the other expenses. I wanted to give something to the girl too. The punishment lasted more than half an hour, every stroke lasting a minute. Finally, the guard carried the bench into a corner, and the girl came into the room where we were. We all moved into another room which had opaque windows where no one could watch us. Anna told the girl to undress, which she did painfully. Her behind was swollen and you could count the slash marks. The skin was broken and long streams of blood were trickling out of it. It was very beautiful.

"Did you only feel pleasure once?" Anna asked her.

"Just once," the poor little thing answered in a low voice. Her legs were trembling and it seemed to me that she desired more pleasure. Anna told her to put her legs on a chair, then she knelt down in front of her and began to play with her fingers in the grotto of pleasure. She thrust her forefinger in between the lips and drew it out again quickly while with her tongue she caressed the top of the font. The girl was breathing heavily and sighed with delight. She had seized Anna's hair with both hands and was pulling it in her fevered ecstasy.

"Are you having a good time?" Anna asked her.

"Oh, yes indeed. Don't stop yet, it's so good. Oh! Oh! Don't stop . . . Slowly . . . Ah! Now if you could bite me, tear me apart! Please . . . "

This sight greatly excited me and I wanted to take Anna's place with the girl. Anna noticed the change in my expression and stopped her play to ask, "Will you try? And you, Nina (she was speaking to Madame de B.), don't sit there like a log, amuse yourself with the young lady." Madame de B. burst out laughing. She stripped and so did I. Anna did not follow our example and for a good reason. A body as spoiled and marred as hers would have taken away all desire to amuse ourselves further.

Nina was still very beautiful; she had an even lovelier body than my mother. She had never had any children, and there were no wrinkles on her abdomen, which was not fallen as it so often is in people her age. Judging by her face she must have been at least fifty years old, yet she was less beautiful. She was not lustful — you would have said a marble statue, quite inanimate. Now, also, she remained completely cold.

I took Anna's place by the girl's knees. As she had interrupted the play of her fingers and her tongue, the spring, which had been ready to overflow, had returned to its bed, and I had to start everything over again and warm her up once more. Nina had knelt down beside me; she had her left arm clasped around me, while her right played in my grotto of pleasure, which was all damp and sticky and burned as if full of explosives. The odor of the girl's cave and the perfume were more pleasant to me than that of the rarest flowers. It made me feel quite drunk.

Anna had knelt down behind the girl and was playing with her tongue in the little opening situated just beside the temple of love, which Grécourt refers to, in speaking of the conformation of the woman, as the "water closet right next door to the country pavilion." This tickling excited the young girl and she writhed about more and more as the spasm approached.

"Oh, my God!" cried the girl. "It's too strong! I can't hold myself back any more! I am going to . . .!"

A burning and slightly salty jet gushed into my mouth. The girl wanted to withdraw herself a little, but I pressed her against me crying, "All! Give me all!" If it had been champagne I would not have gulped it down with more delight.

Thus ended this delightful and unforgettable game. We got dressed and I gave the girl twenty florins, kissed her tenderly, and told her that she need not steal any more, since I was taking her into my service.

III

You asked me not to hide from you any of my experiences or feelings, so I have not hesitated for a moment to tell you about all my depraved desires, however abnormal they may be. I feel sure you will understand me, for you are as profound a psychologist as you are skillful as a physiologist. Most probably no other woman has ever made avowals of this sort to you, but you have surely studied such cases and perhaps succeeded in sorting them out. I am a lay woman and know nothing of these sciences. I acted on the spur of the moment, without stopping to think whether my actions would be repulsive to our better feelings and fill us with horror. Had I been complete mistress of myself and not been swayed by my senses I would have shuddered at the thought of engaging in such filthy acts. But now, having done them, I am of a different opinion, for I cannot see what makes them obscene.

Perhaps you would blame me for this if I were explaining it all to you in person; it is possible too, that you would not blame me. You are better informed than I as to the organic conformation of man and you hold the key to this phenomenon in your brain. I am basing my argument upon my personal experience without being able to guarantee the accuracy of what I say.

Before anything else I have to answer the question: what exactly is meant by "filth"? Every day we nourish ourselves with matter which, when analyzed, is found to be in a state of decay. Try as we may to convince ourselves that we purify our food with water and with fire, it remains a fact that we eat dirt. Certain foods have to be completely rotten to please us. Do not wine and beer have to be fermented before we taste them? And fermentation is to a certain extent decay. Just think what pigs and ducks feed on, cheese swarms with worms, and let us remember the process by which herrings are salted. I saw that being done once in Venice, and I simply cannot talk about it. If it was only known what is added to the sea salt no one would ever eat them again. In a word, dirt is something very relative, and who thinks of the raw materials when he is enjoying something? It is exactly the same as if someone, having fallen in love with a girl, were to lose all his poetic feelings by thinking of the natural needs of his beloved. Personally, I believe exactly the contrary. When a man loves some person or object he no longer sees anything obscene, dirty or disgusting in the object of his love.

These few remarks can serve as an apology for what I have done, driven as I was by the blind desires of my senses. I told you about them at the end of my last letter and this must be enough for you.

What my heart felt later is something quite different and much stranger. You, as a psychologist, will find in it a subject for analysis, for if it is not absolutely extraordinary, it nevertheless must be abnormal.

Recently I read several books on the Greek conception of love, the so-called Platonic love, particularly the work of Professor Ulrich, who lives at present in Würzburg. However, he speaks only of love between men and does not say a word about love between women. What will you say when I tell you that I have never loved any man as much as I did my dear Rose, the girl about whom I told you at the end of my last letter? It is true that physical love attracted me, but there was something else in my heart too, a sort of nostalgia, which I have never felt for any man. It was such a pure love that all other women disgusted me, and men even more so. I thought of no one but Rose, I even dreamed of her. I embraced my pillows, I caressed them, thinking that it was she whom I was holding, and I used to weep and was utterly wretched at not being able to see her.

I did not know in whom to confide. Should it be Nina or Anna? Or ought I to beg Monsieur de F. to set her free? He would of course ask me how it was that I knew her and I should not know what to reply. In the end I decided to talk to Anna about it. She saved me the trouble of introducing the subject in our conversation by beginning at once to talk about the shared pleasure herself.

"It is the only thing which still rouses me," she said. "And today I did not have the best of it. I let you take the supreme pleasure. Aren't you in love with little Rose? Now, don't deny it."

I was still full of complexes and I blushed.

"Ah! Ah! Ah! Is that a blush I see? That is a sure sign that you are in love with the girl, but even if I had not seen your face I would have guessed it when you gave her the money and told her you would give her a job. Three months soon pass, and I think that the girl will indeed prefer to come to you than to go back to prison. As for her desire to be whipped, you can fulfill it just as well. Perhaps she will prefer rods to the whip also, and you will get a lot of pleasure from it too. It is very exciting, I will guarantee you."

"Would it not be possible to get her out earlier?" I asked.

"That would be difficult. She has to finish her sentence. It doesn't really depend on Monsieur de F. to release her, although he has a lot of influence. However, I will talk to him about it."

"Don't tell him my name. He might suspect something."

"Don't worry. He won't be at all surprised by my offer. There are plenty of ladies in the town who do as men do and have lovers of both sexes. I will tell him it is for me. But no, he would not do it for me. I will tell him that there is a lady from abroad who is looking for a girl willing to let herself be tortured and that I do not know of anyone except Rose. At the same time, you must not have her in your house for the first few days. Later on, I will say that the lady has left Budapest and that for pity's sake I recommended Rose to you as a chambermaid."

"But do you think he will believe it?"

"Why not? I have a smooth tongue. The main thing is that he will need a large bribe."

"How much?" I asked her in alarm, for Nina had warned me of Anna's avarice. "How much do you think?"

"Hmmmm. Perhaps a hundred florins, perhaps more. I don't know."

"I would not like to put more than a hundred florins into it," I said firmly. She did not know that I would have given two or even three times as much!

"All right, give me a hundred florins right away. If he agrees to this price, the girl will be with you tomorrow; if not, I will give you your money back. I will go straight to his house now, before he goes off to the casino, but I haven't enough money for a cab, so give me another florin. Of course, I am not asking anything for my trouble. Your friendship is enough for me."

Nina was right. That woman would have taken every penny I had if I had not been careful. I was fully aware that she would go the whole way on foot.

Less than an hour later she was back again. She said F. was making difficulties so she had added another fifty florins and he had given in. He only did it out of kindness. He had not asked who it was for; he had the impression that it was a cavalier, who wanted to remain anonymous. Thus I was obliged to give her another fifty florins. Then she started complaining of the bad weather and people who wouldn't pay up. She showed me a bundle of pawnshop receipts, telling me that she would lose everything if she didn't pay the interest on them by the next day. So I gave her yet another fifty florins. She assured me that she considered this sum as a loan, but I told her she need not return it. I wanted to make sure of her silence and further services, should I need them.

The next day I told the whole story to Nina. She informed me that F. was getting barely thirty florins out of it and that Anna had put the rest in her pocket; however, we decided to have a good dinner as a celebration.

"It is possible that you may be saving a lost woman," said Nina to me. "And God will repay you for this action. But it is going to cost you money, because the girl will need clothes. You ought to get a bath ready for her too. Those poor girls pick up vermin so easily in prison. I had a girl at home about the size and height of Rose. She left me and left her clothes behind. She could afford to do so, since she had stolen mine. Hers will be good enough for Rose. Inspect them yourself and give me what you think they are worth."

Madame de B. was the exact opposite of Anna. I estimated the clothes as worth about forty-five florins, but she would not accept more than thirty-six and I had difficulty in making her take a brooch as a keepsake. She was very disinterested.

It was almost eight o'clock when Rose arrived at the house. I took her to Ofen at once and we had a Turkish bath. It was October and the baths always get hotter as the outside temperature falls.

The poor child was feeling the aftereffects of the previous day's punishment, and I hardly dared touch the places where she hurt. I soothed her a bit by sweeping my warm tongue across them and licking her gently. The warmth of the bath made her very lively, and she was no longer as ashamed and timid as she had been before. She threw her arms around my neck, entwined her legs around my hips, then sucked the rosy buds of my breasts, then my lips, then my tongue. She swore to me that she would never love a man if I would love her as I had shown her the day before. She was wild with joy and told me that it would be the greatest delight for her to be strangled or stabbed by me. The girl was still a virgin, something which I had not dared hope for. I could not manage to thrust my forefinger into her prison of love, for the intact skin of her virginity blocked the way.

"Tear it," said Rose to me. "I don't want it anyway. I would rather love you than a man."

In Vienna Roudolphine had made me a gift of an instrument which I had not yet tried. It was a new invention and arranged so that two women could use it. The pouch which contained the warm milk hung in the middle with two globes protruding from it left and right, so that each pleasure-seeker was at the same time man and woman. It was this instrument which I wanted to try with Rose, so I removed my finger and told her to reserve the best things for that night.

Having taken our baths and allowed ourselves a few relatively unimportant caresses, we went

174

home again. Anna and Nina were already awaiting us. The former had ordered a succulent champagne supper and had brought a long rod, saying that I was going to know that pleasure, too.

The room was well heated so we undressed. Anna did likewise. I did not notice her faded charms, for she immediately crawled under the table, saying that she was going to play at being a dog. She came up between my legs. I had to part them and lean back a little and she took them on her shoulders.

Nina was passing me the dishes and filling my glass. We ate and drank so much that even she, who was normally so cold, was on fire. I threw a few mouthfuls to Anna, although she only ate the biscuits and other sweet things, after having dipped them in my grotto.

After supper, I fastened on my instrument to share with Rose the delights of Aphrodite. The girl was just about to go to bed and was looking for a chamber pot because the champagne was about to come out.

"No! No! That's not what I want you to do," I called to her. "You naughty girl. Are you going to deprive me of the best? You are not to lose a single drop of it. Open your legs at once."

I knelt down at that instant, glued my mouth to her shell.

This preliminary was as agreeable as the principal act, and I was burning and trembling so much with impatience that I could not fasten the instrument. Anna helped me by putting the larger of the two shafts into my shell, where it penetrated halfway. Rose then lay down on the bed, I parted her thighs — for I was playing the role of the man — kissed her, and pushed blindly, but I could not find the entry to her temple. At last Nina put the instrument in position, and I pushed with such force that I broke through the membrane and penetrated to the end. Rose gave a feeble cry. At every movement the instrument penetrated deeper. Suddenly I heard a swishing sound over my head, then felt a sharp pain in my behind. Anna was wielding the rod. She had only given me three blows when the springs were opened as much in myself as in Rose. We were delighted.

"It is a pity you do not have a simple instrument," said Nina. "I shall hardly be able to soothe myself with my fingers. Anna, strike me a few times to excite me. You can't stay quiet with these people in the same room."

I told Nina that she would find an instrument in a drawer of the dressing table. It was one that Marguerite had given me.

Then, the principal scene took place; we formed a group such as the Romans represented on cameos and bas-reliefs. Nina lay down on top of me; my behind was exposed to the blows that Anna was dealing out, and her weight pushed me deeper into Rose. The contact of their two smooth, naked, and burning bodies excited me to the highest degree. We began the joust of love again and this time it lasted much longer. Nina lent more strength to my attacks and Anna was beating us each in turn. The spasm was fast approaching, the blows fell faster and grew stronger, and they were no longer enough for me. I implored Rose to bite my arms and shoulders, calling to her, "Bite until you draw blood!" And she did. At last we climbed the final step and I lost consciousness. The pleasure over, my limbs were tingling. Nina and I were almost crushing poor Rose and our springs seemed as if they would never run dry.

I do not know how long this ecstasy lasted — I shall call it a swoon — but when I came to myself again Anna and Nina had left. The instruments were lying on a chair near the bed, the women had turned the lamp down low, and the room was suffused with a faint light. Rose was sound asleep. Her left leg was around my breasts, the foot and the toes were on my behind. From time to time she sighed. She held me close with her left arm, the right one was hanging out of bed, and the bedclothes were pulled up over us. I did not want to wake her up, so I fell asleep, to wake again well after ten in the morning.

I am not going to tell you about all the scenes in which I took sometimes the active and sometimes the passive role. I should only be repeating myself. You have learned enough about the subject and it would only excite you as I get excited when I read these pages, for I have made a copy of them and it serves to excite me when my senses are relaxed.

A few days later Anna came to see me again. Nina had been coming every day to continue our Hungarian lessons. With Rose, every time we found ourselves alone, I enjoyed every pleasure and we went to the baths together every day. She was as faithful to me as if I had been a man. Even today, after so many years have passed, she has remained for me what she was then, and though she has known the love of men since then, she swears that she prefers to taste love in my arms rather than in the embraces of the stronger sex. I, too, believe that sometimes and I am convinced that if we did not have to perpetuate the human race we could manage very well without men, so strong is the pleasure between two women.

Anna asked me to join an orgy, given on the grand scale every year at carnival time in a brothel. She told me that ladies of the highest aristocracy took part, that they were all masked, and that no one could recognize them. In wearing this mask, they distinguish themselves from the other goddesses of Venus. Everything was arranged in the greatest luxury. Men could come in without paying, but every lady's ticket cost sixty florins.

"You will never see anything like it in Paris. The prettiest whores (Madame de L. always used the most uncouth words and I cannot do otherwise than repeat them — does it shock you?) are invited and about eighty gentlemen. The price is not exorbitant, since about 150 people are there and the tickets work out to about twelve florins a head. The procuress expects only to make up her expenses and the gentlemen only for lost time. There will be lights, music and supper. Last year Countess Julie and Countess Bella paid 1,200 florins to cover the cost. Admission will probably be more expensive this year. I shall have a free entry, as usual, but if you want to take part let me know during the week so that I can have a ticket reserved for you."

At first, I did not want to, for I had already spent far too much money. Rose alone had cost me over two hundred florins. My fees were fairly high, but I would have been embarrassed to spend another eighty or one hundred florins. However, Anna pressed me so much that I finally accepted. Two days later I received a lithographed card with a vignette on it that I had already seen in a French book: a magnificent vagina, half-closed, covered with fur and placed upon an altar, surrounded side and back with ranks of masculine organs with grenadier bonnets and a lock of woman's hair. The cards were signed by Countess Julie and R. L. (Theresa, (Resi), Luft), one of the best known brothel keepers in Budapest, who, as I afterwards discovered, was the protégée of Madame de T.

Anna had told me there would be a masked ball, but ladies wearing masks were not obliged to have any other ladies and, in any case, care would be taken not to cover those parts necessary to the games of love. A picturesque costume would augment their charms. In short, she painted such a glowing picture of the *fête* that I no longer had any regrets, and set to work at once to make an appropriate disguise. Nobody was to know that it would be mine. Madame de B. was about the same size as I, so I told her to have my costume made to her measurements.

One evening Anna came to get me to go visit the brothel where the carnival was to take place. She promised to get me men's clothing so that nobody would recognize me, and I would pass off as a young student. She was such a good talker that once more I gave in and was soon transformed into a young man. My hair was cleverly hidden. My movements and gestures seemed quite natural, as I was used to playing male parts in *Les Huguenots* and in *La Nuit de Bal* by Auber. The weather was fine and the pavement dry, so we went on foot, for it was not far. We crossed the square of the Franciscan monks and took the first turning into Embroiderers Street. It was still quite early and there were no visitors, since they only arrived after the theater. The directress of this pension was a fat woman with very brown skin, and looked rather like a Bohemian. The expression on her face was vulgar and hard. Anna introduced me and the woman stared, and then smiled. I saw at once that she had seen through my disguise and I was already sorry I had come.

"So you want to see the girls, young man. If you had come yesterday you wouldn't have seen anything out of the ordinary, but I have just received two samples, one from Kaschau and the other from Madame Radt in Hamburg. I have a dozen of them now. When I have too many visitors I send for Monsieur de F.'s Julie and old Radjan. She is always happy to sell her outdated merchandise in my house. Has the young man already had a shot (that was her expression)? Does he want a virgin, is that why you brought him to my place?" she went on, addressing herself to Anna. "If that's the case, I suggest Leonie. She only started in the business two months ago and is only fourteen, but she knows more about it than an old one."

She led us into a large room, quite elegantly furnished. There was a piano and the walls were covered with mirrors, while the odalisques of this public harem reclined on divans. Each seemed lovelier than the last, and it was difficult to choose between them. They seemed shy rather than bold. Leonie, a very pretty redhead, had something provocative about her attitude, and something dainty in her features. She wore a rather old-fashioned hair style, and was tall, slim and supple as a sylph. Her neckline gave a glimpse of her breasts, which stretched her blouse almost to the point of splitting. She took care always to show her legs, which were very slim, and her dainty little feet. I sat down opposite her and Anna seated herself opposite us. Leonie pinched my thighs and behind once or twice and showed signs of becoming even more aggressive, but Anna snapped her fingers. I held out ten florins to the proprietress for her to bring us wine and sweetmeats. She looked at the banknote disdainfully and said, "Is that all?" Her words made me angry, but I told her I would pay whatever she liked, though I only had a hundred florins on me. She said she would show me something I had never seen before and walked out of the room, with Anna following her. I was left alone with the women.

Among them I found something I would never have expected. They were well educated and some even possessed knowledge that many an aristocrat would have envied. One played the piano very well, had a very fine voice, though it was not trained, and a good ear. She sang a few arias by Offenbach very tunefully. Another showed me an album of very fine watercolors done in her leisure hours. A few complained of their fate and deplored the ill-luck which had brought them there, but the others seemed perfectly happy. They said the society gentlemen were pleasant company and very gallant, that the students were rude but that it was in their arms that the girls found the most pleasure, for these young men spent their strength without counting.

"What do you expect?" said a pretty Polish girl whom they called Vladislava. "An admirable young man comes here. He is as proud as a peacock, and all the women are in love with him. He went to bed with me one night and before morning he made love nine times. That is a lot with one girl. It is easier to do it once each with a dozen women than five times with the same one. I only know one other man who could do as much, but he has never done it to me. He must have a lover, some rich woman who keeps him."

"You must mean the theater manager's nephew," said Olga, a joyous Hungarian girl. "That is Arpard." When Olga pronounced this name I started. "He is not kept by any woman," went on Olga. "He is rich enough to have a mistress of his own."

"I know that the Countess Bella made him the most generous offers and he refused," said another. The return of the madame and Anna interrupted our conversation.

"If you will come with me, young man, I will show you something to rejoice your eyes. Something really beautiful," she said, pinching my behind. I followed the fat woman down a long corridor and through several rooms. Then she opened a door as gently as possible and put her finger to her lips. The room was in darkness although a faint light filtered through a window draped with white curtains. She took my hand and led me towards a sofa which stood before a glass-paneled door. I heard a faint sound coming from the room next door so I climbed onto the divan to see better what was going on there. The room was well lit and I could see everything, but the two girls who were there could not see me.

Presently an old man came in. He was bald and had an ugly wild beast's face. He was fairly tall and very thin. I could hear every word they spoke. The girl undressed quickly as did the old Caledon, a real caricature of the Knight with the Sad Face. The man was ugly, his thin skeleton covered with a yellow, hairy leather. He was just opposite me. He had a small nose and a shriveled face and I could not see him fully at first, nor could I make out whether he had two navels or two arrows of love, for his sex organ was no bigger than a bean. The two girls posed in positions to excite him, but it was no use, so he lay down on three chairs. They tied his feet and wrists together and one of them began to beat him while the other offered him first her behind and then her shell. The blows fell upon him every minute, and soon I saw drops of blood appear like beads upon his skin.

After ten minutes his ugly rear was covered with bruises and was nothing but a shapeless, bleeding mass. Yet he begged the girl who was treating him so roughly to hit even harder and he sniffed and licked at the openings of the other. Sometimes I heard a trumpet blast or the sigh of an oboe, which seemed to come from the intestines of the girl whom the old satyr was sniffing at. He breathed in the odors through both nostrils. "It won't do like this," he sighed at last. "But give me a sausage and it will come at once, Louise. Will I get a sausage or two, dear Louise?"

He lay on his back and the girl whom he had been smelling sat upon him. The other girl tried to force his feebly rising lance into her hole. I heard the sound of the oboe again and saw what he wished. This filthy operation put him into the desired condition and finally, after a furious trembling of his body, he ejaculated a few drops of sperm.

I very much regretted having been at the
brothel. For one thing, it had proved very expensive, and for another, I could no longer contain
the disgust that had risen in me from witnessing
that scene between the old man and the two girls.
The revolting spectacle brought back to me vividly, however, that I had done much the same thing
with Rose, and my conscience began warning me
that one day I too would need to have recourse
to such stimulants in order to satisfy my jaded
senses. A lover finds nothing disgusting in the
object of his love. But there could be no question
of love in the case of that sated old man. It is
the same sentiment that drove me to Rose and
that drives men to good-looking young boys. In
what strange way did this natural feeling man-
ifest itself in the old man's case? What he procured from total debauchery was, from the aes-
thetic point of view, disgusting.

And I too had let myself be drawn to these
same horrors. I must have temporarily lapsed
into a sort of mental drunkenness when, at the
sight of the mutilated buttocks of Rose, I threw
myself under her to drink the long draughts of
filtered champagne that flowed from her shell of
love, when I exposed myself to the blows of Anna's rod, or when I pleaded with Rose to bite
me! I thought so then. Today I think otherwise.
You know what I have said to justify certain
filthy acts and certain abnormal or perverse desires. However, after having seen that old man,
everything disgusted me from the most violent
and morbid desires to the most natural of relations with a man or another woman. I would have

driven off Arpard if he had come and wanted to make love to me just as I drove off Rose when she came to spend that night in my bed.

I could not forget the revolting spectacle that I had seen, and I spent a very bad night, haunted by nightmares. But, since at ten o'clock that morning I was to be present at a dress rehearsal at the theater, I finally managed to drive away the dark images from my mind.

Among the persons attending the rehearsal I noticed a stranger who immediately made a strong impression on me: a very handsome man, well dressed, with an intelligent face. When the tenor sang a false note, he leaped to the stage, took the score, and sang the passage with such passion and so much expression and taste that the whole cast was enraptured. I have never heard a voice his equal; it sent shivers of delight the length of my spine. Everyone applauded wildly and the tenor cried, "After you, sir, it would be a profanation for me to continue!" And with that he ripped up the rest of his score.

I asked Monsieur de R. who he was and if he was Hungarian.

"You are asking me more than I can tell you," he replied. "His card carries the name Ferry. He could be Hungarian, English, Italian or Spanish, as well as French, German or Russian. He seems to speak all languages. I have not yet seen his papers, and the only thing I know is that he has just arrived from Vienna, that he is received at court there, that the English ambassador has recommended him to his *chargé d'affaires* for something or other, that he has dined with the manager of the royal theater, and that everyone is happy to have him at dinner. I think that he is on some sort of diplomatic mission, and I know that he is living at the *Hotel de la Reine d'Angleterre.*"

Ferry remained to the end of the rehearsal and we were introduced. He was a perfect and gallant gentleman, and I had to watch myself closely when speaking with him.

I was always free in the evening when I had a long rehearsal in the afternoon or morning, and someone had recommended that I go often to the theater in order to hear good Hungarian spoken. So that night I attended a performance accompanied by Madame de F. At the first intermission I had the pleasure of an unexpected visit from Ferry. He excused himself for coming to see me so quickly, but I begged him to stay. He paid me several compliments, saying he liked my voice very much, that I had good stage presence, that my costumes and makeup were excellent, etc., but he never spoke a word of love. He was simple and polite, never common and never importunate, and I resolved then and there to make a conquest of this man before the women of Budapest society got to him. I immediately brought all of my charm and coquetry into play, thinking to win him rapidly and, as he asked permission to pay me a visit soon, I thought that I had already won. I was soon to discover my error.

We finally did speak of love, but in a very general way. However much his eyes were eloquent, his tongue remained mute, and if his words left me in no doubt of how much I pleased him, he never so much as hinted at asking the slightest favor. When he pressed my hands upon arriving or leaving, he did it almost nonchalantly, without attaching the least bit of significance to it.

Finally, even so, I managed to steer the conversation to his past loves, and I asked him if he had made many conquests and if he had ever been seriously in love.

"I take the beautiful where I find it," he replied. "I believe that it would be an injustice to bind myself to a single individual and I think, in theory, that marriage is the most tyrannical institution in society. How can a man of honor dare to offer that which does not depend solely on his good will? Generally speaking, I believe that one should never promise anything to anyone, and you will never find a soul that can say to you truthfully that I have once promised him something. I do not even promise to come to a dinner when I have been invited; I content myself simply with acknowledging the invitation. I never gamble; chance is too great a power for me to give it the opportunity to defeat me. And that is why I never promise a woman to remain faithful to her. She must take me as I am if she takes me at all. If she is willing to share my heart with others, she will find plenty of room. That is the reason that I have never yet made a declaration of love to a woman; I always wait until she tells me simply and frankly that I please her enough so that she can no longer refuse me anything."

"I imagine that you have already come across many such persons," I said to him, "but I cannot understand how you have been able to love them. It seems to me that a woman must be extremely imprudent to dare take the first steps in an affair, without waiting for the man to assume the initiative and make the overtures."

"And why, may I ask?" he replied. "Does not a man prefer a woman that loves him enough to dare to break all the laws of conventionality to one that simply plays a role? Women who demand the man's initiative are only going to give in at last in any case. A man infinitely prefers a woman who knows how to sacrifice her vanity to a woman who only knows how to be a coquette. Bitterness often pushes a man to revenge himself on a woman who has made him languish a long time, and when she finally cedes to him what he wishes, he will be unfaithful to her and leave her."

"And those unfortunate young women that cede to the first attack of the man, do they also merit his vengeance?"

"I have never revenged myself but on coquettes, and I would certainly not like to seduce a young, innocent girl. I have never done it either, although God knows I've had the opportunities. Each woman that I have had has offered herself to me without my asking anyone to sacrifice her virginity. Each of them was free to choose, and they said to themselves, 'Should I prefer him who pursues me and who does not please me, or him who pleases me and says nothing?' And each of their choices fell upon me. They managed to free themselves from the foolish scruples that their mothers, aunts and other frustrated spinsters had taught them from childhood, and they played their game in the open. None of them ever regretted it, for each knew the risks she was running; I explained to each one that, though she could possibly become a mother, even so I would never marry her, that I loved other women as well as her, and that she might never see me again. Tell me, was I honest or not?"

I could not deny it, but I also told him I would never dare to make a declaration of love to a man.

"Then," he said, "you will never love a man. For love in a woman entails sacrifice, and I will never show the slightest favor to a woman that will not give me the proof of such a love."

He had answered everything I had asked; I knew now that he would never make a declaration of love to me. However, it was evident that I pleased him. Why else did he visit me so often? He preferred to be in my company rather than go out for the evening. Nevertheless, I hesitated. I wanted to make the declaration he wished, but I wanted to do it in such a manner as to save myself as many blushes as possible, and I hoped to find a means during the carnival. I didn't know if he thought me experienced or not but, in any case, virginity obviously had no particular charm for him. What he would have liked would have been a virgin as corrupt as a Messalina. Unfortunately, there are no such virgins.

I did not know if I ought to confide in someone and have them act as an intermediary. I finally talked to Anna. She told me that although Ferry had already succumbed to another woman, she would do everything possible to win him for me. Above all, however, she wanted to know if he were going to participate in the orgy which was to take place in the brothel.

Several days later she brought me the news that Ferry's mistress was the Countess O. Her chambermaid had overheard the initial conversation between the two. He had proposed exactly the same conditions to the countess, adding to the two that he had mentioned to me as being necessary — that the woman must make the overtures and that she must not count on his fidelity — a third: that each woman who gave herself to him must be completely nude. When a woman accorded everything to a man, he asserted, there was no reason for her not to reveal herself completely. The countess had accepted.

I do not know if I could abandon myself in that fashion, even if I were to be in love. I am very liberal on that point; however, I cannot free myself from a certain prudishness which, innate or acquired, still dominates me. I have not yet learned whether this facet of my character is common to all women.

In the meantime, Anna told me that, though Ferry would undoubtedly participate in the orgy, as he had been invited by three women, he had not promised definitely, for it was against his principles.

The evening of the orgy approached rapidly. Anna, Rose and Nina helped me to finish my costume and try it on. It was made of a sky-blue silk, very heavy, with insertions of white gauze and brocaded gold flowers. My buttocks and, in front, my breasts and my belly, from the navel to three inches below my grotto of delight, were uncovered. On my feet I was wearing a pair of crimson velvet-tipped sandals. My collar was the ruffled lace one sees in portraits of Mary Stuart. The sleeves of my dress were elbow length and embroidered in gold. An Indian shawl, also in gold, was fastened about my waist and my hair was adorned with multicolored marabou feathers.

I did not want to wear my own jewels, as they would have given away my identity, so I left them with a Jewess, who lent me some others. Besides this, I carried a staff with a gilded penis in erection on its tip, and wore a mask that covered my whole face except for the mouth and eyes. The color of my hair was not unusual enough to betray me, although there were very few women who could claim locks as rich as mine. In all, my costume was in very good taste and quite original.

The 23rd of January, Anna and I went to the house on the Goldstickergasse, I wearing a heavy cloak over my attire. When we arrived, Anna left me in the vestibule and I was received by Resi Luft. Although the hall was already well filled and the orchestra playing, the first men I saw upon entering were Monsieur de F. and the baron. They were almost entirely nude, wearing only a sort of skimpy bathing suit in clinging silk, and they wore no masks. My entry, meanwhile, had created a sensation. I heard the women murmuring, "There is the one that is going to beat us tonight! . . . My, she is pretty! . . . That one is made of sugar, and how I would love to eat some of it! . . ." And the men were even more excited. The most beautiful parts of my body — my breasts, my arms, my calves, my buttocks, and my sex — were all bare or scarcely veiled. I waited not a second, taking the opportunity to seek out Ferry immediately. I finally found him dancing with a woman dressed in white tulle scattered over with roses and lilies, for she was supposed to be a nymph. Her body was fairly well proportioned, but not as beautiful as mine. Another woman had her arm around Ferry's hips. She represented Venus, and the only articles she wore were a belt of gold, a few diamonds and a crown in her raven black hair. She held the great, erect scepter of her partner in her hand, and I must admit that I have never seen as large nor as handsome a lance as his. It was of an extraordinary size, as red as the sandals that were the only clothing of its master, and it shone as if it had been dipped in oil. The rest of Ferry's body was a gleaming white, tinted here and there with pinks and roses. Not even an Apollo, a Belvedere or an Antinous could have been as handsome or as well proportioned as he, and I trembled at the sight of him. My eyes were so busy devouring him that I stopped involuntarily before the tableau of which he was the center. His Venus had a very pretty body, very white, but her breasts were slightly pendulous, and her violet-lipped grotto was too open, too ravaged by love.

Suddenly Ferry's eyes found and rested on mine. He smiled very slightly and said, "Very good. That is much the best method by which to take the initiative." He then broke away from his women and came towards me, bent his head down to mine, and whispered my name in my ear. I blushed scarlet beneath my mask.

The orchestra, separated by a great screen from the revelers, broke into a waltz, Ferry took me by the waist, and we whirled into the maelstrom of couples. The contact of all those bodies, burning and brilliant, male and female, infatuated me. All the members of the men were fully erect and, during the dance, turning towards a common goal. Kisses bubbled everywhere, and an exquisite perfume began to float upwards from the closely clasped bodies. I was dizzy with joy. I felt Ferry's dagger touch me suddenly, butting its head like a maddened bull against my sex. I pressed myself against him, spreading my legs so that he could enter lower down, but he did not attempt it, asking me instead, "Are you ever jealous?"

"No!" I responded quickly. "I want to see you like Mars with Venus."

He left me quickly and took Venus, who was dancing with another man. Meanwhile two of the girls of the house, Vladislava and Leonie, brought out a stool covered with red velvet and placed it in the middle of the room. Venus bent over it, leaning on it with her hands, and Ferry attacked her from the rear. Vladislava and Leonie then knelt at the feet of the combatants, the first spreading Venus' lips, the other tickling Ferry's testicles. Ferry gave Venus such a riding that she was soon groaning in ecstasy; I was now feverishly stripping myself. I now stood entirely nude before him and asked, "The mask too?"

"Keep it," he said and, withdrawing his rod from the goddess, shooed her off with a smack on the behind so that I could take her place. My knees turned to rubber. Ferry then kneeled before me, tonguing me so masterfully that I thought I would surely discharge; finally he attacked me from the rear as he had my predecessor. I noticed then that his rod was the splendid rose color of the symbol on the staff I had carried to the ball.

It was too much! Venus and another woman were sucking my breasts, a third was kissing me and thrusting her tongue between my lips to suck and bite, while Leonie was kneeling between my legs and tickling the base of my font with her tongue. My senses whirled, my breath rasped in my throat, and my whole body trembled; everywhere hips, thighs, arms and buttocks burned me, and from my font flowed a whirling stream like whipped cream, jetting into the mouth of Ferry, who drank it to the last drop. Then he leaped to his feet once more with a bound and drove his great scepter into me to the root. All my nerves, which before had been distended, now knotted with desire; my temple of pleasure was on fire; the shaft of stone ravaged me like a knife. How that man could ride in the joust of love! Sometimes he completely withdrew his weapon, rubbed the head against my lips, then thrust it in again suddenly and violently. I could feel the tiny opening of my hymen attempting to absorb the enormous head of his mace; it held it tightly, as if in a vise, until he completely tore it violently open. He repeated this game several times, his movements accelerating and becoming more abandoned, while his rod expanded even more. He was no longer master of his desires, and he leaned heavily upon me. His fingers bruised my thighs, his mouth sank into my shoulder, and his tongue sucked the blood. Suddenly I felt his jet inundate me and overflow my sex.

I thought that I had lost the game, that all was over, but at once he began afresh, his weapon a prisoner in my cavern of joy, regaining its vigor little by little. He kept up the assault and I responded with ardor. The duel continued, but more carefully, more slowly, to the applause of the spectators, who had now formed a circle around us. Thrust followed thrust at regular intervals; I suddenly felt an electric shock that nearly paralyzed me — a great jet even more scalding than the first ripped through my body.

Once more he was to prove his strength to me, his love and his virility. The spectators became delirious when they saw him withdraw his sword from the scabbard for the third time and for the third time thrust it back in to renew the combat of love. They began to cry, "All good things come in threes!" This time the game lasted a good quarter of an hour and they watched it to the end. Ferry was indefatigable, but the crisis had to arrive sooner or later and our joy was infinite. He inundated me with his sperm, carrying our passion to undreamed of heights. I was no longer standing on my own feet. Several of the girls of the house were supporting me, while from all sides, I felt nothing but nude flesh. Women were covering me with kisses and biting my nipples, while Ferry, still standing behind me, clasped me in his arms.

Finally they left us alone. Ferry clasped me once more and then offered me his arm to take me to another room. "On the throne! On the throne!" cried several voices, for there had been erected at one end of the hall a sort of throne made of an ottoman covered with red velvet and surmounted with a canopy of purple. It was there that they wished to carry us in triumph, to indicate that we had won first place among all the combats of love. Ferry declined in my name, thanked them for the honor, and said that if it were permitted he would prefer to take a short rest. Thereupon the woman who was dressed as Venus took us into the banquet hall, but the table was not yet prepared.

"Isn't there a private room somewhere where my Titania (he called me thus, for he said that

I was most beautiful of the beautiful) can rest quietly for a minute?'"

"Resi Luft ought to have several," replied Venus. "I will tell her to ready one for you." She disappeared and soon returned with our hostess. At sight of her, we burst into gales of laughter, for she had followed our example and was completely nude. She was old, enormously fat, and incredibly greasy, a perfect twin of that famous queen of the South Sea Islands, Nomahanna. Oh, those great reddish rolls of flesh and that timber forest beneath her belly! But somehow she proved appetizing yet, for I understand that she found several men to taste her charms and to let themselves be swallowed up in that set of flesh.

She let us into a small room near the dance hall, from where we could watch the progress of the bacchanal. There were several couples still dancing, but most of them preferred a more serious occupation. We could hear the murmur of voices, the sound of kisses, the panting of men, and the sighs of women. I was sitting on the knees of my lover, and becoming more and more excited by what I could see, when something hard and hot rose against my buttocks. I did not need to guess what it was.

"You are not ready to start again?" I asked him, covering his mouth with kisses.

"And why not, may I ask?" he said, laughing. "But would you refuse if I shut the door and asked you to remove your mask? I want to be able to see the sensuality and the pleasure in your face."

He was not the tyrant that I had thought. This despot of mine was as mild and caressing as a shepherd. I went to the door and shut it. Then I turned, took off my mask, and threw myself on the bed. I spread my thighs, pushed myself up on my elbows, and awaited my cavalier. He didn't hesitate a second before ramming home his lance, and this time there was no one to disturb us. I saw only him and he saw only me.

Can I possibly tell you what I felt? No, I think not. It will have to suffice to say that we drank three consecutive libations to the gods of love, and I simply cannot tell you the joy I felt at having these all by myself and in privacy. When the crisis approached, his eyes fixed themselves on mine and took on a savage expression of desire. We rolled breast to breast, stomach to stomach, arms and legs entwined like serpents. At the end, we lay side by side, his scepter still inside my case, our eyes closed, resting and finally falling asleep. We lay in this ecstasy a good half-hour until the sound of the revels reaching their peak awakened us. I dressed hurriedly, forgetting my mask, which Ferry took and put on my face, and we reentered the hall.

The orgy had indeed reached its height. You could see nothing but groups of bodies, in every imaginable pose, made up of two, three, four and five persons.

There were two groups that were particularly complicated. One was composed of a man and six women. He was lying on his back on a plank across two chairs. He was running one girl through with his lance; another was sitting on his chest while he licked her grotto; his hands were tickling the fonts of two other girls; the remaining two were being invaded in their sensitive spots by his big toes. These last two were actually playing less; they were there only to complete the group and had to pretend to be satisfying themselves.

The other group was composed of Venus, who was stretched across one man who invaded her from the front, while another attacked her rear, an opening much smaller than the first. In her two hands she manipulated the organs of two other men. The fifth man, a giant from Rhodes, knelt on two chairs above the head of the first, who sucked his shaft of love. The climax was achieved at the same time among all six of them. It was undoubtedly the best group.

A third group was made up of two women and one man. One of the women was lying on her back, the other on the stomach of the first with her legs tightly wrapped around the hips of her partner. They were both spread voluptuously, biting and licking each other. The man dressed like Hercules, forced his lance first into one and then into the other, and I was curious to see how they would share his vital fluid when the time came. As it turned out, it was a reasonable and just division; neither received more than the other. When the crisis struck he did not lose his head, but doled the nectar out equally. The one on the bottom received the first.

Every man and woman at this ball took part in the activities. No one remained a wallflower. Everyone was a combatant at least twice, and Ferry among the men and I among the women were in the best form.

Venus, the Countess Bella, and I were the only women who had so far remained masked. Later on I learned that Venus was a woman famous for her affairs and I discovered her identity. She never, however, removed her mask. However, the Countess Bella was a veritable fury, a female demon. She cried in a loud voice, "Look! Look! Don't you know that I am a whore, a real whore!" She then made a tour of all the ladies of the house, giving them candy, fruit or champagne. At the table, she drank a full tumbler of brandy that a man had poured for her and rolled dead-drunk onto the floor. Resi Luft dragged her into a room and locked the door, while Bella tried to break it down. Finally she went fast asleep. Later, two of the whores went to see if she were still sleeping and found her flowing from every opening like a leaky barrel. They put her on a bed and she slept until four the next afternoon.

The supper was in every way worthy of the orgy. Several persons slept on the table, and there were not more than two men besides Ferry who were capable of comporting themselves decently. The others were left standing by, hanging their heads sadly. Finally the prizes were distributed. Ferry was proclaimed the king, followed by one who had played the harmonica very well, and a third who had given out a lot of candy. My chief rival, the Princess O., whom I had found in Ferry's company, had finished him off very well. I tried to get him to drink until he was drunk, thinking that it was a chance of reviving him, but he refused. However, he did down one more glass of brandy before the orgy terminated at four o'clock in the morning.

Ferry and I, Venus and several other women went home. The rest were drunk and passed the remainder of the night at Resi Luft's.

On the whole, I noticed that the girls of our hostess conducted themselves better than the other women. They had been asked to take part in the ball by the men beforehand and all continued into the bacchanal that followed except Leonie. However, it was said that she was actually a member of the nobility, and that she had left her parents, members of an old Viennese family, to come directly to Resi Luft and practice her adopted *métier*.

Ferry accompanied me to my apartment, where Rose was still up awaiting me. She did not go to bed until I finally asked her to, and need I tell you that for Ferry, who was himself again, and I, the war of love was not yet over for that night?

V

Perhaps you are becoming irritated because I seem to be telling you nothing but the things that happened to me in Budapest, and perhaps you are accusing me of loving the Hungarians to the exclusion of all others. I will say, therefore, that in certain things, the arts for example, and I place love among them, no one country can be predominant or claim the prerogative. However, there is no country in the world whose inhabitants are more skillful in the art of intimate dalliance than Hungary. They are at least as advanced as the French and Italians, the grand masters of this pleasant pastime, and one could even say they are superiors.

And I think I can prove it.

A short time before I undertook this correspondence I made the acquaintance of an Englishman who had been traveling to all corners of the world for over forty-four years and who had seen — at one time or another — every country.

My friend, for it is thus I shall call him, had just come from Italy and he described to me a house of the priestesses of Venus that he had seen in Florence. The three most sought-after women of the house were Hungarians and their prices ran into thousands of lire. When the madame of the house decided to reform her establishment, she made two-thirds of her new students Hungarians. There were also some Spaniards, several Dutch girls, a Serb and an Englishwoman, all of whom were more beautiful than the Hungarians, but none of them could play their role with men like the latter. And it is the same everywhere, from Paris to London and from St. Petersburg to Constantinople; even in the German cities the Hungarians are always preferred.

Not only have the women of this country carried off all the prizes of love, but the young men also. These young Adonises are nearly always strikingly handsome and display captivating manners. They are somehow different from the men of other nations, and that difference is what attracts us. Finally, they are untiring when playing the game of love, and they seem to know every refinement. With one of them for a partner, a woman need never employ an unusual stimulant.

Do not think, after all that I have just said, that I have an exclusive passion for the Hungarians. I am going to tell you of the many other experiences I have had with men of all countries, so I shall now return to my story.

I was splitting my pleasure, during those days in Budapest, with two persons, Ferry and Rose.

The former was my declared lover while the latter served to vary my excitements.

One day Ferry surprised me by saying that until he had met me he had never known real love, that his long-held principles were no longer as solid as they once had been, and that he could now admit his fidelity. If I wished, he added, he would now consent to marry me. Despite the allure of such a proposition, I refused and was forced to refuse many times again when he continued to put the proposition before me. I was too afraid of killing our love by attaching other bonds to it, for I firmly believe that both the church and the state have made marriage a tomb for love. The memory of the happy life of my parents did not serve to reassure me, for I felt that that had been pure chance. Very simply, I loved and the secret of our pleasures only served to augment my love. Ferry appreciated and finally adopted my views.

I was, however, somewhat disturbed at the possibility of becoming a mother and losing my place on the stage. I finally confided my fears in Ferry, professing astonishment at the same time that I had so long escaped pregnancy despite the fact that I had thus far completely neglected the precautions that Marguerite had so strongly recommended and which I had always employed with the prince.

There are many other means besides that, Ferry told me, and said that he had been using one all along without my knowledge. "There is a book called *The Art of Making Love Without Fear*," he added, "and I will give you my copy."

I read very carefully the author's remarks on many things. First of all, he did not recommend the use of the condom. He claimed that it was only a hindrance to the complete pleasure of the man and woman and said that since it is not made to measure, it will be painful to the man if too small and will form wrinkles if too large, as painful as a hair caught inside, to annoy the woman. There is also a very good chance that it will break. Besides all this, it is a dirty and disagreeable operation to dispose of it after the act is finished.

The author also said there was only one chance in a thousand that the woman would conceive if the man entered her while they are standing and attacks from the rear. The head of his rod, in this case, is not exactly opposite the cervix, and the semen enters the vagina but not that dangerous little opening which spreads so wide when the woman discharges her liquid. The author also added that it takes a certain amount of time for the semen inside the man's body to become potent, and that after two ejaculations it is no longer dangerous for a long period.

At this point I remembered that Ferry had almost always taken me from the rear, and that he had only attacked from the front after two or three times from the other direction. Had he done it expressly for this reason?

I also learned that urine tends to neutralize the effects of the sperm and I knew that Ferry, who was not always confident of the frontal position, often used this means to save me, an act which, by the way, increased my pleasure enormously.

The author made a fine distinction between the sperm of a man and his semen, saying that there was no difference between the sperm of the male and the female and that it was not the semen which caused his excitement, but the sperm. For otherwise, he asked, how could the woman, who possesses no semen, become excited and know happiness? In fact, the sensuality of the woman is much stronger than of the man precisely because she does not have any semen. He went on to explain further, but it became too complicated for me and I did not understand. I remember that we two have often talked of this same subject, and you also insisted that after several ejaculations the male semen was no longer fertile. This explains why the people of the north, who have a colder temperament, multiply more rapidly than those of the south, who are more passionate. The Hungarians, the French, the Italians, the Orientals, and the southern Slavs have much fewer children than do those of the north, and particularly the Germans. Their strict habit of marriage is much more fertile than is the freer conduct of the south. In the same way, the lower classes are more fertile than the aristocracy. (Later I read Klinkossols and Venette, both of whom said the same thing.)

The author recommended several means of avoiding the dangers of pregnancy, one of which was the following: the man, when approaching his crisis, should withdraw his shaft from the woman and let his semen flow onto her stomach or thighs. Where, I ask you, is the man sufficiently master of himself to be able to do this every time? And besides, does not this practice thwart the principal goal of the love act, for is not the ultimate aim of the lovers to feel mutually the electric shock which the discharge of the semen produces inside the woman? I detest the man that would continually practice this method of contraception. I myself know of two methods which I have often employed successfully instead of the condom and which, I admit, are really too clumsy. These are the silver ball and the sponge.

A heavy silver ball with a thin piece of elastic attached to it is introduced into the grotto and, since it is heavy, falls to the bottom blocking the opening of the cervix. This of course, prevents the male sperm from entering there. It is much more practical than the condom and also serves as a stimulant, for each time that the shaft of love touches it the ball is embedded a little and produces a most delightful tickling. If the ball is heavy and well-polished it is practically impossible for the shaft to dislodge it, thus keeping risks down to a minimum. Also, the elastic band makes it quite easy to remove when the time comes.

The use of the sponge is based on much the same principle. The sponge should be large enough to cover the whole of the orifice of the temple of desire, so that there is no chance of it being moved accidentally, but it need not be particularly thick. The woman of course is in no danger of conceiving because the sponge absorbs all of the semen. The vagina scarcely becomes wet.

These means are particularly efficient when the man's rod is not too long and does not reach the end of the vagina. At each movement by the partner, the sponge trembles and quivers, exciting the most tender and sensitive parts of the grotto's interior, and in order to increase the delight even more one may smear the surface of the sponge with wax in order to roughen it a little.

This reminds me of a woman who could never find a man able to satisfy her. So one time an officer among her lovers fitted himself with a special ring, which he attached so carefully just beneath the foreskin of his penis that she did not notice it. The ring was made of rubber, but notched in the form of teeth. Thus armed, the officer bent to his task. The rubber performed its duty so well that soon the woman was completely ravaged and bleeding inside. It was extremely painful but provided her with the stimulation she needed. Unfortunately, he could only employ this efficient weapon very occasionally because of the damage it caused.

The book related many more means of safe intercourse, but I am sure that you know them all. In Hungary the most widely employed method was the use of a concoction made from the saps of a tree called the Sabine's Needle (*juniperus sabina, I think*). All of the peasants used this method, but it is very dangerous and I know of several cases of poisoning that resulted.

However, I must get back to the subject of my adventures.

Untroubled, because of the contraceptives I was using, I abandoned myself completely to love. I loved no one but Ferry and, thanks to his prudence, no one suspected our relations and my reputation did not suffer in the slightest.

Rose, however, had much to complain of. Ferry took no notice of her to speak of, and I rarely had a night free to spend with her. Realizing this, and since I was not a victim of any kind of jealousy, I asked myself if it would not be wise to push her into the arms of Ferry also. The taking of her virginity with the aid of my rubber instrument that night had not been completely successful, for the membrane had resumed its former position and she was once more as good as new. As a doctor, you are probably going to say this is impossible, but I assure you that several months after the episode with Anna and Nina I attempted to insert my finger into her cavern and found my way blocked. I made her lie down on the couch and examined her grotto very carefully under a lamp. She spread her legs and I saw an entry that was completely round, with a little partition that was quite hard and completely inelastic. It reminded me of the presentation of a virgin at the panopticum on St. Joseph's Square near the fair of Budapest . . . I am not religious and I am only telling you what I saw.

I asked Rose if she would like to have a lover like Ferry, and she replied that when she had me she did not want any man. She said that if she had to sacrifice her virginity to a man she would be doing it only for my pleasure. Ferry did not seem to her any more desirable than any other man she had known.

Very few women know the pleasure of watching the combats of another couple and very few men feel anything but scorn for a woman who gives herself to another man before their eyes. Ferry and I were exceptions.

Ferry had often asked me to give myself up to another man before his eyes, but I had always refused, thinking that he wanted to quit me and that he was only looking for an excuse. I had not yet begun to believe that it was only pleasure he was after. However, he told me of many examples of the same thing, citing in history the cases of Gatta and Melatta, the Venetian heroes who never made love to their wives until they had abandoned themselves to another man. Finally I was convinced, and we decided that Ferry should teach the art of love to Rose and that afterwards I would do the same with a young man.

I had a great deal of difficulty in convincing Rose that she should take part. She threw herself into my arms, crying and saying that I no longer loved her, and I had to try to prove the opposite. I kissed and sucked her front, I bit the nipples on her breasts, I excited her so that she panted with desire. Then Ferry helped me to strip her and soon she was nude before us. Ferry kissed her tenderly and passionately, stroking her foaming grotto with his shaft of love until finally the moment arrived. He picked her up and carried her to the bed where he placed several pillows beneath her behind. She spread her legs involuntarily and he kneeled between them. The little fake was trembling in all her limbs, but she had her eyes closed so that we should not see how much she really wanted the pleasure that was about to come. I kneeled on another pillow so that her head was underneath my stomach. She immediately pressed me with her left hand while her right held tightly to Ferry, to whom I had turned my stern. When Ferry finally broke through Rose's membrane she bit me violently. Even this pain was wonderful. Neither Rose nor I could prevent from crying out in ecstasy; Ferry alone was silent.

Rose was so violent in her pleasure that Ferry could hardly stay aboard her. She bucked, groaned, then cried out passionately or cooed like a dove. We lay there, one on top of the other, one within the other, and our burning bodies smoked in the bed. I forced my nose deep into Rose's armpit and lay there, drunker than if I had been drinking all evening. Our ecstasy was infinite.

Little by little we recovered and left the soaked bed. Ferry advised us to take a bath at once, which we did. In Budapest, I had made a hot bath a daily luxury, for I found that it always revived me immediately, no matter how fatigued I was by either love or work, and it did no less for us this time.

Ferry was a master of love. He knew every means for increasing and renewing pleasure. And this time he was no less imaginative. When Rose and I got out of the tub and began to dry ourselves, he stopped us and told us instead to rub soap and oil over our bodies. This we did, and our bodies became as slippery as those of two eels. Then he had me lean over the bathtub while he hoisted Rose to his shoulders. In this position, with her facing him, he attacked me from the rear, not through the ordinary tunnel, but through a neighboring one that up until then had been virgin to me. He had smeared it well with oil, making his entry much easier. However, it did hurt a little.

While he was thus occupied, he put his arms around me and forced his fingers in through my cavern and I could feel his hands inside me almost reaching his shaft. Only a thin layer of skin seemed to separate them. Sensuality was, at that point, much stronger than pain and I was completely ravished by desire. In the meantime, Rose slipped onto my shoulders so that her temple of love was now before my mouth. The game was exquisite and we all came at the same time. However, Ferry would have finished his play much sooner than either Rose or I if he had not kept his head. For he was forced to stop and remove his arrow from my quiver several times in order to remain master of himself. Each time that he returned to the assault a sharp pain which quickly turned to a quenching sensuality filled me. It was thus that he attacked five or six times before we were all reduced to intoxication. Rose's fountain overflowed its banks. In the meantime the flow from Ferry's weapon inundated my interior and my own source sprang forth.

I can never remember having had an experience like that again. It was undoubtedly the height of my sensuality and I will never be able to forget that game in my life. We finally parted and went to Rose's bed to sleep, for mine was still afloat. We lay down, Ferry in the middle and the two of us pressing on him from both sides.

Ever since that night I have never been able to understand jealousy in women. It no longer seems to me reasonable and natural that these things do not happen more frequently in our civilized countries, for I am convinced that copulation and desire have for their object, not the perpetuation of the species, but simply the experiences of sensuality.

The very next day Ferry reminded me of my promise and assured me that if I carried it out no one should ever know. He told me to accompany him on a short trip.

It was spring and the weather was magnificent. Ferry told me we would leave Budapest on the day after the next, and he spent the intervening twenty-four hours entirely with me.

We left the city on a Sunday at two o'clock in

the morning. Taking Ferry's private carriage instead of a train or boat, we traveled the rest of the night until we reached Nessmely around eight in the morning. There we left the main highway, crossed Igmand, and arrived at around noon in the famous forest of Bakony. At an inn in the middle of the forest we found a table already prepared for us. There were several rather sinister and evil looking men about, and I thought that they were perhaps robbers. Ferry talked with them a few moments in Hungarian and I asked him worriedly what they were up to. He told me that they were just some poor devils that lived in the wood, and that I had nothing to fear. In the afternoon, after we had eaten, we climbed back into our coach, this time preceded by five horsemen.

We no longer went as fast as we had, for the road was very bad and narrow. Finally we arrived at the densest part of the forest and once more alit from our carriage. We walked the rest of the way and the coach was driven to a building which I could barely see through the trees and which looked like an inn. The horsemen preceded us, parting the branches for our passage, and we finally reached a beautiful glade with a large and deep stream. We rested there and ate, and an hour later, two men appeared. One was about thirty-four or thirty-five and was built like a Hercules. His face was savage but very regular, almost handsome. The other, scarcely twenty, was as beautiful as Adonis. Ferry presented the two men and told me I would now taste the thrills of love with them, that I had nothing to fear, and that neither knew who I was nor had the slightest relation with the outside world.

The Hercules immediately stripped, but the young man blushed and hesitated. Ferry gave him a sharp command and he followed suit. I undressed slowly and Ferry told me that I should abandon myself completely, because the more passionate I was the more pleasure he would take in the sight. However, knowing his thoughts, I resolved to be as dissolute as possible. I called the two men and took them by their lances. The little mushroom of the young man immediately became a branch of oak that reached all the way up to his navel. The giant's sword had unsheathed itself as soon as I had undressed. I took the young man's weapon and started to tickle the end of it but as soon as I touched it I received the full flow of his burning discharge. In the meantime, the giant lifted me by my buttocks until my behind was touching his stomach and, without my guiding him, thrust his lance straight into my shell. I thought he would penetrate right up to my throat, his weapon was so long. His blows fell slowly, measuredly and powerfully, and I thought at each shock that I would swoon. However, I never loosened my grasp on the young man's shaft and it soon grew hard and strong once more.

"Is it good?" Ferry asked me. He was not yet undressed himself.

I could only reply to his answer with my eyes. I almost fainted with delight and my lock gates began to open wide until they finally released my precious nectar, flooding the giant's great shaft. However, he continued without tiring, and worked a good half hour before he began to feel his crisis approach.

"Don't give her any children!" cried Ferry, laughing.

"Don't worry! Where I'm going to end up you'll never find a baby growing!"

And with that, he removed his redoubtable staff from my shell and I thought I would die from pain when he forced it into the neighboring hole. He gave only two thrusts when the juice from his loins flowed in a jet that lasted at least a full minute. It repaid him well for his long labor and finally he withdrew his dart. It was covered with blood — my blood — for he had so skinned me that I could not at all sit down and scarcely walk. He carried me to the stream and washed my wound with his fingers, thereby soothing my pain, but I still could not walk a step. I was very sorry not to have accorded the young man more pleasure, but I had solaced him twice.

I remained about an hour in the water, then the giant took me in his arms and three men helped him dress me. They finally took me into the house where Ferry put me to bed.

Can I describe to you vividly enough the three days that I passed in that forest? I changed lovers every day and even more often than that, for there were nine brigands. And the third day we celebrated with a great orgy with the peasants from nearby. Agrippina would have envied our saturnalias. These peasants were as skillful and adroit as the aristocrats of Budapest.

I had plenty of time to rest up during the rest of my vacation and Rose alone accompanied me. I left Ferry after many tender farewells, but it was necessary, for many more debauches would have surely killed me.

I have nothing more to say of the remaining two years I spent at Budapest, nor of my one-year engagement at Prague. I have learned to appreciate this famous French saying: "Neither always nor never; that is the motto for love."

VI

I was twenty-seven years old. My parents had died some time before within a week of each other, carried off by an epidemic, and I was for all practical purposes alone in the world. The rest of my family had either died or lost contact with me. Of those I knew about, my old aunt with whom I had lived in Vienna had lived the longest; she died about a year after I left Budapest. The cousin I spoke about some time ago decided to follow a military career. He completely lost that bad habit of his youth and became such a räke that debauchery finally killed him. For myself, although I had been very lucky in most things, I had to bear several bad turns. For one thing, I had lost both of my first two lovers. Arpard was employed indefinitely at the embassy in Constantinople and Ferry had emigrated to America. The only one who remained to remind me of my joyous days in Budapest was Rose.

I am not going to bother relating the progress of my artistic career, for if you are interested in it, which I doubt, you can surely find all the information you want simply by opening the newspapers.

In one of the large German cities I got to know an Italian impresario who had heard me sing in a concert recital and an opera. He paid me a visit one evening and asked me to come to Italy. He said that since I spoke perfect Italian, the only thing needed to help me compete directly with

the greatest Italian sopranos was for me to spend
some time on the stages of San Fenice, La Scala,
San Carlo and the others. If I were successful in
Italy, he said, my future and glory would be assured. I was supposed to begin at the Pergola in
Florence. The offer was so good that I signed for
two years.

I risked less in Italy than anywhere else for
there no one bothers in the least about the private life of a single woman. That particular
feminine virtue that is held so much in honor in
the rest of Europe has no value whatsoever in
Italy. There, they worry more about the conduct
of a married woman than of a single girl, which
I find very reasonable. When a woman has reached the age when she has already experienced all
the nuances of love, the Italians do not worry
about her past life. No man expects his bride to
be a virgin if she is over fifteen.

For myself, at twenty-seven I had reached the
apex of my physical beauty. Everyone who knew
me in the days at Vienna or Frankfurt said I
was much more beautiful than I had been at
twenty-two. I had a robust nature and a very
forceful but fiery temperament. However, I always had the will to master my desires when I
felt they were about to undermine my health.

At Frankfurt I had spent two chaste years and
after leaving Budapest I again restricted myself,
even limiting my pleasures with Rose. She was
wonderful about this, never attempting to provoke me once. In fact, she seemed always to have
exactly the same sentiments and feelings as I,
and our accord was often as perfect as that of
two Siamese twins. I always kept a journal (for
how otherwise could I have ever been able to re-

count the smallest details of my life?), and as I leaf through it now, I find that after my relations with Ferry ended I enjoyed in the period of five years, the pleasures of the body with Rose only sixty-two times, or an average of once a month. How do you like that for temperance? And furthermore, during this period I did not have relations with any men. I was in good health, I lived well, I took care of my body and committed no excesses.

At Florence, I met a very interesting man whom I have already mentioned, the well-traveled Englishman. He was no longer a young man, being fifty-nine years old, and I knew I could talk about anything with him. He was a discriminating epicurian and a student of human nature, and most of his opinions were very close to my own. Thanks to him, I learned to know myself better than I ever had before, for he explained many things. For example, I had known for a long time that the natures of man and woman are completely different, but I had never known why. This remarkable man was able to give me clear physiological and psychological reasons.

His philosophy of life was clear and simple: it is impossible to undermine one's principles if they are based on reason. He was not cynical, and in society he was taken for a very moral man, although he did not profess a single virtue. He paid a sort of gentle court to me, not in order to gain what most men seek, but because I was willing and capable of listening to and understanding what he had to say. However, I realized that he would have been very happy to possess me physically, for that is entirely natural. I am not a female Narcissus, but I know that I have a very good body. I only have to look in the mirror and compare what I see with what I see on other women to know that. And you have told me that you never saw as well proportioned a form as mine, and this many years after I knew Sir Ethelred Merwyn.

I was even a little annoyed to hear this Englishman sing my praises so continuously without ever attempting to attack my heart — or anything else. The word heart is only a euphemism. However, my coquetry was in vain. He had explained many things to me, but I still wanted to know why he was so platonic with me.

There is a proverb that says, "If the mountain will not come to Mahommed, Mahommed must go to the mountain." Sir Ethelred certainly resembled a mountain in this case, and it soon became evident that if I wanted any results I would have to become a prophet.

"Since I permit you every familiarity, Sir Ethelred," I said one time, "why do you never go beyond the most formal politeness? I know very well that you have been a great Lovelace in your time from what you have said, and I am sure that you still make the occasional conquest."

"You are mistaken, Madame. I am no longer in the field for making conquests," he replied. "You do not think that an old man like me is going to charge about in pursuit of seductive young ladies? It would only be frustrating and bad for my blood pressure."

"I am not talking about chippies and light women. You are not answering my question. Do you take me for a heartless coquette that only wants to hitch you up, with all the others, to my triumphal chariot? Don't you think you could inspire love in a woman of my age?" I insisted.

"I suppose it is possible. However, if you accord me your favors it is undoubtedly out of pity and not out of love. Besides, it would be a foolish desire on your part. You have known nothing but young men. I believe you just want to see me looking ridiculous."

"You are being unjust towards yourself and towards me. I told you once of a man I knew who did not deign making conquests, who waited for women to offer themselves voluntarily to him. Do you have the same vanity? Are you waiting for the same thing? You should take advantage of your situation. If you make advances towards a woman and they are repulsed, you can say it is because of your age. If you succeed, all the better. However, a woman may be deeply humiliated if you simply follow her, playing the role of chaste Joseph. Too much timidity and too much modesty do not go to make a man."

"However, it is even less becoming to him if it is said that he is an old satyr," he replied.

"You are still a handsome man and you possess many qualities that make one forget your age. Forgetting all prejudices against my sex, if I told you that you could hope for every favor from me, that you could demand anything, would you not decide to accept?"

"That is impossible. You would never do it."

"In any case, can you tell me if you would refuse or not?"

"I would be crazy to refuse. Of course I would accept," said Sir Ethelred.

"But you distrust me at the bottom of your heart. You think I am like another Messalina."

"Not at all. The taste and the capriciousness of

a woman are absolutely inexplicable. If you said something of the sort to me I should undoubtedly love you, and that love would make me the happiest of mortals."

This was a complete contradiction to what he had said a few minutes before. I moved close to him, slipping my hand through his arm and looking up at him so tenderly that he would have to be made of stone to resist. I detest coquettishness when it is nothing but a weapon of vengeance or conquest, but Sir Ethelred had always been my friend and I had no reason to attempt to vent my spite on him or make a fool of him. I would not like to say that I loved him either, but it was certainly possible that more intimate relations might reveal that sentiment. I finally pressed him so that he forgot his principles, fell at my feet, kissed my knees, and slowly became more enterprising. I did not offer the least resistance. He put his right arm around me, while with his left he played under my dress. Then as his face approached mine I did not even await his first kiss — I gave it to him. At the same time, I opened my thighs, thrust my abdomen forward, and made everything easy for him to find the temple of love.

These preliminaries had, meanwhile, excited me so that he found my grotto hot and humid. In all this time he had not said a word and I thought I saw a tear shine in his eye. He no longer seemed to believe what was happening to him. I eased myself from his arms to shut the door, then I told him that it would be better if we went to the bed, that he undress and help me do the same. You should have seen my Englishman when he finally saw me completely nude. I believe he thought he was dreaming. He knelt before me and kissed each part of my body slowly and carefully. Finally I began to undress him, something he had not at first wanted to permit; he gave in, however, when I told him that it would give me great pleasure.

I could not understand why he had been so timid with me, for his body was really very handsome. His shaft was strong and fiery, and his skin was fine, smooth and white without the smallest trace of splotchiness; on the contrary, it was still tinted with the reddish shadows one finds on a young man. I lay down on the bed and he again knelt before me, kissing my grotto which, at the touch of his tongue, opened impatiently to receive its guest. Sir Ethelred knew also that the first ejaculation is dangerous, for when it was ready he withdrew his organ, clasped me again in his arms, and discharged at my side.

"Do you still doubt me?" I asked.

"I believe I am dreaming. I never dared hope for such happiness, and I still do not pretend to understand. I only know that I am your slave, that I can never refuse you anything."

Sir Ethelred had already made more than one excursion into the domain of the gods of love, and he passed the time very well while waiting to regroup his forces. I helped him with my fingers and my mouth until finally his weapon was again in form. I did not want to be left again halfway down the path, so I did not let him resume the attack right away. Finally, when I saw that his desire was almost painful, I offered myself in sacrifice. This time he lay on his back and I sat on top of him. I held his two hands and worked over his shaft with my grotto, rubbing against it without ever letting him enter. The poor man shut his eyes, sighed and panted until, at the moment when he was least expecting it, I threw myself on his scepter. He opened his eyes, but I immediately lifted myself so that his shaft came out, and he had to press it up after me. I amused myself for several minutes like this, and then our movements became more regular. During these exercises I began to use the muscles of my cavern so well that sometimes, even when I raised myself, his rod remained imprisoned. This is a trick that is very popular with men and it served to inflame his tool even more than before. I could feel that his crisis was fast approaching and I accelerated my movements even more in order to open my own lock gates at the same time. Suddenly the storm broke, and I noticed that his eyes became strangely fixed, his movements more violent, and he began to pinch my buttocks and bite my shoulder. I received his jet a few seconds before my own fountain began to flow, but then I returned his liquid with interest. I was almost swooning with delight when suddenly I was brought back to myself. The strange rigidity and immobility of my lover startled me.

For a second I thought that an attack had killed him, for he did not reply to my questions. However, I put my hand over his heart and felt it beating doubly fast. I quickly slid away from him, feeling his cutlass leave its sheath and something hot run down my legs, and took a glass of water from the table to bathe his face. The shock revived him, he sat up in bed, looked around the room, and then embraced me violently and kissed the blood from my shoulder where he had bitten me. He was very embarrassed and I had to calm him while we dressed. However, his weapon seemed to say that he had not had enough, because it was standing at attention beneath his shirt, so much had I excited it. He would have accepted a third bout of love, but I felt that he had had enough for the time being. I have heard that certain persons have suffered attacks while making love and that it happens more often to men than women. That would be terrible, to suddenly find oneself embracing a cadaver.

Sir Ethelred seemed to have guessed my thoughts, for after we went into the garden he brought up the subject.

"So you do not know to what excesses sexual passion can carry one? There are many cases on record where men have violated corpses. The law would not forbid such a thing if it did not exist. I don't know if it happens more now than it used to, but I know there are still many instances of it. During the Napoleonic wars this passion often had serious consequences for its victim, and I remember a particularly strange case that occurred just before the battle of Jena. A French officer was staying with a Protestant pastor whose daughter had just died; that is to say the doctor in attendance had filled out a death certificate. In reality it was nothing but an acute case of catalepsy. The girl was supposed to be interred shortly after the departure of the officer, but the soldier, seduced by the beauty of the corpse, violated it. The shock of the copulation caused the girl to revive shortly thereafter and she had even, unknown to her, conceived a child.

Her parents were, of course, very happily surprised to find her returned to life the next morning, but somewhat shocked to learn later that she was with child. And the poor girl did not even know who the father of her robust and healthy little boy was. The whole thing was explained several years later when the officer happened, by chance, to be in the village again. The affair made a big stink in the village, for, although the man sought to excuse himself by claiming that he had done the thing in order to revive the girl, it was obvious that this was not at all the case. And the French have many similar cases on their consciences. Nowadays the practice is particularly frequent among the members of the aristocracy rather than among the poor, and of the several instances I know, I will tell you that of the Austrian minister, the Prince of S.

"He used to bring selected corpses to his apartments, ostensibly for studies in anatomy, since he was a dilettante in medicine. However, the doctors at the hospital from which his victims came discovered his practice when a virgin who had died came back in a different condition than that in which she had left.

"This passion is very dangerous for those who practice it, and can even be fatal, for the poisons generated within a cadaver are very powerful. Onanism, sodomy and the violation of corpses are all very common and highly developed. The recent trial of a salami maker caused a sensation when it was discovered that he not only killed his victims, but was in the habit of assaulting them both before and after. And when a woman is executed in Italy, which is not a rare thing, you can be sure that twenty-four hours after her death her body has been violated. This is so common that in the rare cases where a husband has never been able to sleep with his wife, he can arrange to do so after her death. This practice is also current in France and England, particularly London, where the police are badly organized and inefficient. The greatest crime that a man can commit is to mutilate himself, but have you ever heard of it being punished?"

What Sir Ethelred told me filled me with horror. For him, automutilation and the violation of cadavers were only bad and dangerous habits that could do harm to those addicted to them. The law should neither punish automutilation, the violation of corpses, nor attempted suicide. Laws should punish only those crimes that are likely to be harmful to others.

What he told me made me tremble. These things were too morbid to be possible; I could not believe in them.

"It would be easy for me to convince you that these things really go on if I did not fear that I should change your feelings for me. All I would have to do would be to take you to the places where they happen."

"Where? Here in Florence?"

"No, not here, but in Rome. I can show them to you when you are there to sing."

"All right. I promise that my love for you will not suffer because of what I might see and that I will be strong enough to stand the sight of such things, but you must promise that I will never have to take part or be exposed to one of the assassins. Also I would not like to see anything where a person is mutilated for life, for those victims should offer themselves only voluntarily. I don't want to have to sit through scenes like those described in Sade's books."

The time, meanwhile, passed very quickly in the company of so gallant a man. We were very temperate in the act of love, for although he was always ready for new frolics, I was afraid that excess might dry up his spring too soon, and I loved him too much and wanted to spare him this humiliation.

Finally we went to Rome and on the third day Sir Ethelred said all was ready. He had paid an immense sum in order to satisfy my curiosity. On the evening when all would be revealed two executions by garroting were to occur. A bandit from Abruzzi and his wife, a ravishingly beautiful woman, were to be strangled at the Piazza Nivona. Sir Ethelred had rented a window near the gibbet and through his glass I could see all of the muscular contortions of their two faces when they were killed. I suffered cruelly watching this and could not forget those two pitiful faces. Sir Ethelred read my thoughts and said, "You will see them again."

Much later he took me to the "della Assunzione." The orgy was to take place in the church itself and the stones of the floor had been covered with mats of rushes for the purpose. The time was summer and the night was warm. A box had been prepared for us to watch the orgy.

Every sort of act was performed, women with men, men with each other and women with each other, and men with small boys. There were also many animals: a calf, some dogs, monkeys, mandrils, baboons, and some cats. They would stick the animals' heads into a shoe and abuse them in this position.

The last scene in this orgy, the last, for I could no longer stand it and asked Sir Ethelred to take me away, consisted of a double violation of the bodies we had seen earlier.

I stayed fifteen days in Rome, when my great friend was suddenly stricken ill with malaria and died. I stayed with him until his last breath, and I finally closed his eyes. In his will he left me all his fortune, including the stones and antiques he had collected on his many voyages.

This sudden death disgusted me with Italy and I was happy to sign for an engagement at Paris in the Italian Opera there.

VII

It was by chance that on my arrival at Paris I received a sudden confirmation of what Sir Ethelred had told me concerning the violation of corpses, namely, that it extended through all levels of society. The rich practice it out of degeneration and the poor out of necessity, for only thus can they gratify their desires inexpensively. There is an advantage in the fact that a corpse will never betray you. Also, I must admit frankly that a handsome cadaver is probably less repugnant than a grossly ugly living body. I suppose that if one could surmount the first fear and revulsion brought on by contact with a cold, stiff body a feeling of sensuality could arise.

The two famous cases that caused a revolution in public opinion are certainly widely known, even though the newspaper accounts were somewhat incomplete. The trials, however, were practically public and at them I saw women from the highest aristocracy sitting next to women who are little better than those on the streets.

I will tell you, therefore, what I was able to learn about these two dreadful affairs. The trials were held at the same time even though the crimes were committed at different dates, for one of the criminals was a member of the aristocracy whose family had succeeded in keeping the thing quiet for a long time, until the newspapers got hold of it and some new witnesses came forward. The other guilty one was a man of the people who was quickly imprisoned and immediately judged. In the first case, not only was violation uncovered, but assassination as well, and not only on one individual but on several. Two different people were involved, the assassin was one and the satyr another, but the connection between the two was known.

In this trial the following came out: At the Faubourg Poissonniere lived a *charcutier* who was well known for the quality of his meat pastes, and his shop was always full of customers. However, rumors eventually began to get around about his meat, even to the point where it was whispered that he was using human flesh. An investigation was eventually launched and it was discovered that he actually had not been using ordinary meat, but dogs, cats, squirrels, sparrows and other beasts. This revelation stopped the rumors for the time being, but each time his pastes again came into vogue they started again until finally the police and the public no longer paid any attention to them.

About eighteen months after his arrival in Paris, a hairdresser had been arrested for having cut the throat of one of his customers. Investigations indicated that this man had killed several people before and had sold their bodies to his brother-in-law, who was the charcutier. The flesh of these corpses was supposed to have been ground up, but no proof could be obtained. However, at the official interrogation the hairdresser said one of his partners had in fact done all the killing, and had been furnishing the bodies of young women first to a rake among the nobility who was in the habit of abusing them and afterwards to the charcutier for meat. The Attorney General immediately arrested the rake, but he had been following the trial all along and had time to hide all traces of his complicity. Bits of bone and splotches of blood had meanwhile been found in the basement of the second hairdresser, but nothing could be definitely proven against him, and he too was given his liberty.

Six weeks after my arrival, a morals agent surprised an employee of the morgue in the act of violating the corpse of a young woman who had drowned in the Seine. He was quickly condemned to spend ten years on a convict ship, a sentence that was denounced as much too strong by newspapers and public alike and which was reduced to two years at hard labor.

However, the principal result of this second case was that it reawakened public interest in the first, and the newspapers again played it up in a big way. The charcutier, meanwhile, thinking himself safe from any new investigation, shielded as he had been by the rake and the hairdresser, grew careless and found the police one fine day searching his shop, where they discovered the corpse of a young girl of ten. A medical examination established that the girl had been violated, but it could not be determined whether before or after her death.

The charcutier was condemned to the guillotine for murder and, for a long time, denied having any accomplices. However, at the Court of Appeals, when it became apparent that nothing else would save him, he admitted that he and the hairdresser had been furnishing the corpses to the Duke de P., who paid twenty gold napoleons apiece for them, adding that it was the duke who had originally talked them into the affair. The duke, of course, denied any knowledge of the affair, although he later admitted that he had been violating the corpses supplied to him, and that he had known they had been murdered, probably for him. His lawyer succeeded in having him arraigned for nothing more than violation of the dead, punishment of which was incomparably small in relation to his actual crime. The hairdresser and charcutier were found guilty.

I never saw such a circus of love as existed at Paris. The inhabitants were so enervated by pleasure that I do not think they ever tasted natural copulation, and among the demimondaines I think there were some who never even attempted to look for pleasure.

I met one of these women once, the mistress of the Russian Prince Demidoff, a woman of rare beauty. She was about thirty-three, but I would have thought perhaps twenty-five at the most, had I not known. Her lover spent huge sums of money on her, but he also made overtures towards me. However, I told him to give up hope of winning me and he did. I possessed a respectable fortune in my own right, thanks largely to my dead friend.

The Russian was very ugly, over fifty, wore

a wig, and dyed his mustache. I have always mistrusted people who try to hide their age; Sir Ethelred had gray hair and I think he would have been ashamed to wear a wig.

In Paris I again formed good opinions of the Hungarians I met, of which there were four: Mathilde, who was the natural child of a prince and sold by her mother to a rich cavalier. She later freed herself and married a rich Parisian banker. The second, Sarolta, a colleague of mine at the *Théatre Lyrique*, was as charming as she was naive. She played a lot with men without ever giving them anything, for she was afraid of becoming a mother. The third was a certain Madame de B., wife of a Hungarian colonel. She had lived with him in bigamy, for he had never divorced his first wife, until the day when the original showed up. He then fled to Constantinople and joined the church of Islam. The fourth girl was called Jenny, the daughter of a Budapest lawyer. She and her three sisters now lived off the commerce of their charms. They had begun their trade by charging medium prices, but a count fell in love with her and started the fashion of going to her house. She and her sisters had had a great deal of luck in their chosen profession and she was counted among the most elegant women of the gilded bohemia of Paris. An Italian cavalier later married her, but he died in two years. She then became involved with a sovereign prince, who literally worshiped her.

VIII

Sarolta and I had decided to go to London. I had lived quite simply in Paris. I was very prudent in love and never once neglected to use the prophylactics of which I have spoken.

I must mention the man who, but for your help, would have caused my downfall. I have never met a more obstinate man. I made his acquaintance about three months after my arrival in Paris, where he had the reputation of being the biggest rake in the capital. He followed me everywhere, even coming to London and staying in the house opposite mine. I thought at first that he was mentally deranged in loving me to such an extraordinary and exaggerated degree until I realized, to his misfortune, that his behavior was nothing but a result of vanity and vengeance. By then it was too late for me.

I loved him until his twofold treason was exposed. In the first place, he made me neglect my usual prudence, and then he contaminated me. In London he did not dare pursue me openly for I could have called for the police, nor did he dare to attack me as he did later in another country and in other circumstances.

Sarolta and I rented a pretty house in St. James's Wood, next to Regent's Park. It was the beginning of the season and the weather, as usual in April, was magnificent. Our cottage was surrounded by a little garden with fruit trees in it, an arbor, and carefully raked pathways. We used to walk there every afternoon after lunch. Our room commanded a wonderful view of Regent's Park.

One morning Sarolta was in my room, and we

were eating a cake by the open window, feeding the crumbs to some robins. A faint, light breeze was stirring the trees and the smell of lilacs was intoxicating. I was in my nightdress and leaning on Sarolta's shoulder when she said: "Look, isn't it strange to see such a smartly dressed gentleman in the company of five or six urchins?" Near a clump of trees in the park, I saw the gentleman in question holding two barefoot, wretchedly dressed little girls by the hand. He was leading them towards a place I knew well, one of the loneliest in the park. He struck me as a pervert who wanted to seduce those poor children, a thing that is no rarity in London.

I waved to a policeman, who happened to be passing, and told him what I had just seen. He immediately dashed off in the direction we indicated. Soon he reappeared accompanied by the gentleman, whose clothes were disarranged, and I followed what was going on between them.

The policeman was arguing with the man, while several little girls stood around them, children of about five to nine years. They, too, were chattering nervously. One of them walked towards the smallest one, then pointed at the gentleman and would have pursued her demonstration further had the policeman not prevented her. A crowd soon formed, and I heard passers-by shouting, "Take him in charge!" A second policeman then arrived and the group moved off in the direction of Marylebone police station.

A few days later we read the gentleman's name in the newspaper. The policeman who had arrested him and the little girls were the witnesses. We went to the hearing. What the little girls said was quite piquant. He had told them to undress and made them lie down on the grass. Then he had licked their youthful grottoes. She had been paid four shillings. Despite this, the accused was not condemned, for he was a wealthy business-man and was allowed to leave after a severe reprimand by the judge.

English laws, justice and the public in general are fairly lenient in these respects, and I can recall many cases which I would have judged quite differently. It was one of my favorite pas-times to read the police reports, particularly the offenses against public decency. Englishmen seem to have a particular art for exciting women, always attempting to display their organs before them and generally indulging in clumsy exhibi-tionism. A young Englishman jumped out naked at his landlady's daughter when she came in to clean his room and nothing happened to him, but a young Frenchman who was slightly tipsy stole a kiss from the same sort of person and was condemned to six weeks' imprisonment. A heavy penalty for a kiss!

The tribunals are especially indulgent with clergymen. There was a vicar who had two young girls boarding in his house and who taught them all sorts of immoral things. He used to take them into his bed, play with their shells and put his member into their hand. The jury condemned him to hard labor, but the Bishop of Canterbury took him under his protection and the judgment was suspended pending a new trial. The two little girls had to appear in court again — their ages were twelve and seven — and it was easy to confuse them. As if two children could seduce a full-grown man! They were sent to Holloway Institution while the real culprit, the Reverend

Hatdret, was set free. Yes, and because he had been two or three weeks in prison he was looked upon as a martyr, a collection was taken up on his behalf, and he was appointed by the church to a very good position.

You know my opinions on this subject, on what people call obscenity and debauchery; you know that I do not agree with the opinion of the majority. I believe that every person — man and woman — is free to do as he wishes with his body so long as it does not impinge on anyone else's liberty. It is a punishable offense to use violence, to seduce through promises, to excite the senses for the same result, or to use narcotics which destroy the will. As long as I have tasted of love and while I have practiced all sorts of pleasures, I have never obliged anyone to submit to my will in these matters.

I stayed three years in London although my engagement was only for two years. However, I renewed it because I liked it very much.

In France, Italy and probably in Germany, crimes are committed just as they are in London — for the sake of pleasure. The most frightful case I know is that of a young Italian named Lani and a French prostitute. He had strangled the girl at the moment of reciprocal ejaculation during the height of ecstasy, then he had continued violating the corpse. Some English lawyers told me that if he had not robbed his victim also — for he had taken her jewels, her watch, and her money — and if he had not bought a ticket to escape to Rotterdam, which made it look as if the crime had been premeditated, he would not have been accused of murder and condemned to death. The strangulation of the prostitute at the moment of ecstasy is ranked as manslaughter and is not punishable by death.

As there can be no degree to the death penalty, it is dreadful that it should so often be applied. There is no justice in it as it stands now. Lani was much more guilty than one of his compatriots who, in a jealous rage, killed his rival just as the latter was leaving his adored one's bed. He then tried to shoot himself in the head but only smashed his jaw. The greatest care was lavished on him to save his life, yet later he was hanged for his crime. This is cruel and barbaric.

I am now closing this list, already too long, of London crimes to tell you of a few of my own adventures there.

I met the sister of that Jenny R., whom I mentioned in my last letter. She was a member of the *corps de ballet* at the Drury Lane Theatre. She was quite pretty and Laura — that was her name — was quite lucky too; one of the wealthiest cavaliers of Prussia, Count H., fell in love with her, made her his mistress, and later married her. The count was no longer a young man and at his death he left her one of the largest estates in Hungary, Presbourg.

Sarolta was not so lucky as she had expected to be. She left London in August, and I was left with Rose. I was invited into the fashionable world, but I was bored with it and yearned to know life in London's gilded bohemia. By luck, I found a letter of introduction from my dead friend to a woman cousin of his who lived in the suburb of Brompton. I sent her Sir Ethelred's letter and my visiting card and received an invitation to her home that same evening.

Her name was Mrs. Meredith, she was about

forty-five, had once been very pretty, and had obviously tasted life well, for she was quite faded, her hair was gray, and her face was lined with wrinkles. She used a lot of powder to hide them. Her philosophy seemed to be epicurian, she had a very good sense of humor, and was rich enough to give parties and move in a circle of well-known ladies, all of the aristocracy. These women were distinguished by their liberty of conduct and freedom of spirit, but their galas and evening parties never ended in orgies.

Despite our difference in age, we soon became good friends. In our conversations, I admitted that I had had intimate relations with her cousin, which she found praiseworthy. She said Sir Ethelred had spoken of our relationship by letter, but he had never mentioned my name for he was most discreet. Mrs. Meredith spoke frankly of these things and even admitted that she had not yet given up love herself. "However," she said, "It costs me quite a lot. My God, I am as bad as those people who are so ancient they have to buy the favors of young ladies. Mind you, I do not believe this dishonors the buyer in the least. It is the other party who is giving the most and receiving the least."

As this woman went everywhere, I had a very good chance to learn some remarkable things about London. The English have a very curious attitude towards theater people and Bohemians. They do not ordinarily receive them in society, or if they do, they treat them like automatons; they are very polite towards them when they are on stage, but after the performances they act like they no longer exist. However, if a cavalier should marry a woman of the street, her past is immediately forgotten and she is treated like a great lady. She may even, if she is the wife of a lord, be received at court. I personally know three women in this very situation.

Mrs. Meredith related many of her adventures at London balls and asked if I would like to visit some of them in her company. I of course accepted. We visited all of them and I observed the character of the Englishwoman. The first thing I noticed was that the woman of this type in England was much more dignified than those in other countries. There were many that were just as depraved as the worst French prostitute, that were equally ready to do anything for money, and there were those also made of marble, ready to rob any man — women with no sentiment and less sensibility. However, in general, the English prostitute I found less insolent than either the French or the German, even those of London. I must admit, to my shame, that the German prostitutes are the most common and vulgar of all. They have to be as they are not nearly as pretty as the English girls and they have to rely on their insolence to force on men what their charms cannot attract. They are always easy to recognize by their loud make up and heavy walk.

Mrs. Meredith had a very pretty country place at Surrey, not much farther from London than Richmond. She invited several young girls out there. I came, accompanied by Rose who, at twenty-six, was as pretty as when I first saw her. Our group consisted of about forty persons and the orgy was supposed to last some three days.

"We are," said Mrs. Meredith, "out to surpass anything that men have done with this orgy!"

A stream ran through the gardens of Mrs.

Meredith's estate. The garden itself was surrounded by high hedges. These acted like curtains and we were completely hidden from any prying eye; we could do anything we wished.

The first thing we did was strip. Then we put on sandals to walk about the garden. The stream bed, however, was of fine sand and we spent nearly all our time there, splashing and swimming. Need I tell you the other things we did also? There is too much to relate, it would make my letter twice as long. It is saying enough to relate that we literally bathed in sensuality. Several of the women even said they had never tasted such delight in the arms of men. Homosexual pleasure of this type is, indeed, very violent and strong. I can understand why women in Turkish harems never found themselves bored, and why they were never unhappy when waiting to be called to the sultan's bed. I now realize they must have passed their time in the same sort of sports that we in the garden engaged in. I even believe that homosexual pleasure is greater for a woman than heterosexual pleasure because she can abandon herself completely to all delights, knowing there is no danger in doing so.

None of us enjoyed these games more than our hostess, and we tried to show her our gratitude by covering her with caresses. The third day we were already so exhausted by our efforts that we had to spend the fourth in bed. The following morning we left for London.

If I had wished to conquer a lot of men, I could have made enormous sums of money while in London. Lord X. for example, was a music fanatic who spent immense sums of money on actresses. He made the most attractive offers through intermediaries; however, I refused all of them as I had all the others.

Despite my relations with Mrs. Meredith, I soon acquired the reputation of being unapproachable.

One time I was invited by a well known woman to the marriage of her daughter, and she proceeded to compliment me as much on my virtue as on my singing. She also spoke to me of Mrs. Meredith.

"Unfortunately," she said, "the good woman does not have a very nice reputation. You have no doubt heard nothing of it, but I think that you knew her cousin, Sir Ethelred Merwyn. It is even said by the gossips that he was your lover, but of course one does not listen to tales such as this. Did he recommend you to Mrs. Meredith? I suppose he had no idea that she was so depraved; however that need neither touch nor worry you, and you need not pay any attention to it."

How that opinion seemed ridiculous! And they also called Sir Ethelred a stoic! I was the only one who could really say, for none of these women had known him like I had.

I took a Hindu boy into my service in London, a lad of about fourteen who was extraordinarily beautiful. I took him because he pleased me a lot and I wanted to initiate him into the mysteries of love. I found a great deal of pleasure in arousing in him sentiments of which he was as yet unaware. As he learned, he developed so that in each muscle of his face, in each movement of his body, love spoke. He became my voluntary slave and there was never any doubt as to the sincerity of his devotion. I often saw him with his eyes closed, lost in his thoughts and his dreams. He would not hear me approaching and would not notice me until I took his hand.

That is all that I now have to say to you. You know everything that happened to me after that, and I shall fill you in on the very recent events when we see each other next. This letter is, therefore, the last.

THE END

La Lolita
Faustino Perez

Blending manipulation and revenge, this justly famous tale set in exotic Mexico features the luscious Lolita, a young woman whose beauty can turn men's minds to madness.

$3.95

The Altar of Venus
Anonymous

Being the true history of a Victorian gentleman who successfully devotes his life and talents to the vigorous pursuit of pleasure.

$3.95

Three Times a Woman
Anonymous

This is the first modern edition of a novel generally considered to be one of the best written works in the annals of erotic literature.

$3.95

Rosa Fielding: Victim of Lust
Anonymous

The story of the beautiful Miss Rosa Fielding and her amorous adventures is a memorable, and often joyous tale of sexual self-indulgence in mid-Victorian England.

$3.95

Secret Lives
Anonymous

This fluent and immensely readable volume of classic Victorian erotica explores the secret lives, the hidden places behind the 19th Century British facade of propriety.

$3.95

The Lustful Turk
Anonymous

The infamous account of a Victorian lady's captivity in a harem is based upon a true incident. The astonishing story of the Lady's initiation into harem life and how she comes to be a willing participant in its amatory adventures, is told by the Lady herself in a series of vividly depicted episodes.

$3.95

Autobiography of a Flea
Anonymous

Probably the best, but certainly the most famous erotic novel ever written.

$3.95

AVAILABLE AT FINE BOOKSTORES EVERYWHERE
OR
ORDER DIRECT FROM THE PUBLISHER:
CARROLL AND GRAF PUBLISHERS, INC.
260 FIFTH AVENUE
NEW YORK, NEW YORK 10001
ADD $1.25 for postage and handling.
N.Y. State Residents please add 8¼% sales tax.